I0657205

HALF-TAIL RISING

HALF-TAIL RISING

BRETT WIREBAUGH

RESOURCE *Publications* · Eugene, Oregon

HALF-TAIL RISING

Copyright © 2019 Brett Wirebaugh. All rights reserved. Except for brief quotations in critical publications or reviews, no part of this book may be reproduced in any manner without prior written permission from the publisher. Write: Permissions, Wipf and Stock Publishers, 199 W. 8th Ave., Suite 3, Eugene, OR 97401.

Resource Publications
An Imprint of Wipf and Stock Publishers
199 W. 8th Ave., Suite 3
Eugene, OR 97401

www.wipfandstock.com

PAPERBACK ISBN: 978-1-5326-8340-4
HARDCOVER ISBN: 978-1-5326-8341-1
EBOOK ISBN: 978-1-5326-8342-8

Manufactured in the U.S.A.   APRIL 17, 2019

Dedicated to my best friend Holly who never stops bringing me joy.
Thank you for your help and support of this project. I love you more!

Also dedicated to McKenna, Carson, Allayna, and Brooklyn
for demonstrating the Windmaster's
love on all our family adventures together.
In exchange for this dedication,
maybe you can stop teasing me for my love of deer now?!!

"But when he saw the wind, he was afraid,

and beginning to sink he cried out, 'Lord, save me.'"

—*MATTHEW 14:30*

"God, the Lord, is my strength; he makes my feet like the deer's;

he makes me tread on my high places."

—*HABAKKUK 3:19*

CONTENTS

If you had been in the Gomer Middle School library that day, you would have no doubt missed a student huddling in the corner, hiding under a hooded sweatshirt. He quietly typed at a little-used, out-of-the-way computer. It had *not* been a good day. Who are we kidding? It had not been a good year. He was feeling especially sorry for himself. But somehow typing the following sentence made him feel slightly better.

```
nobody likes me
```

He was staring through watery eyes at the blinking cursor when he was interrupted by the only person in the school older and crazier than the principal—his secretary. Mrs. Edith Krantz barged into the library, pointed her walking cane at him and squawked with way too much pleasure, "The principal will see you now." The student was so surprised by the intrusion that he accidentally left the message on the screen for anyone to see.

1

TROUBLE

"He makes lightning for the rain,
and he brings forth the wind from his storehouses."

—*JEREMIAH 10:13 (ESV)*

Two tan manila folders sat front and center upon Mr. Vanderflunder's desk, staring up at the old school principal. The only sound in the room was the tap-dancing of his skeleton-like fingers upon the wooden surface, and the muffled sniffles of a boy whose face was buried in a pair of much younger hands. Another boy also sat across from the headmaster, but he waited in bored silence as if the principal's office was a place very familiar to him. The two folders corresponded with each of the boys, not only in location, but also in size. The contents of the folder that lined up with the teary-eyed student were very small, much like the sixth grader whose name was scribbled at the top. Plopped down on the left-hand side was both a folder thick with papers, and an eighth grader thick with size and attitude. At the top of his folder, written in faded, shaky Sharpie was the name Steele Canis. Scratched upon the top tab of the other newer and brighter folder was the name Dolby Hart.

Like a door creaking open, a tired voice broke the silence. "Even though you are new to this school, you are not new to trouble, are you Mr. Hart?" Dolby sheepishly looked up through tears at the old man, and then accusingly to his left at a smirking Steele. "In just two short months, you have managed to visit me no less than five times. What do you have to say about that, Dobby?" Mr. Vanderflunder, as was his practice with names, mispronounced Dolby's to rhyme with Bobby. "Dobby?"

Steele happily corrected him. "It's pronounced Dolby, Mr. V. You know, kinda like 'Dough-boy?'" He chuckled in Dolby's direction, and then made a threatening face. The insult was lost on Mr. Vanderflunder, but not on Dolby. He had only attended Gomer Middle School for two months, long enough to become Steele's favorite victim. Unfortunately, Dolby almost immediately got on Steele's bad side, and he has not let up since. The nickname Dough-Boy was especially hurtful because even though he was smaller than most kids his age, he was also wider than most. The worst part was that Steele was actually right. His body was quite flabby and doughy, which made him terribly insecure. At least he hadn't teased him about his flaming red hair yet.

Fighting back tears, he volunteered, "It's actually pronounced 'Dole-Bee', sir." Steele waited for Mr. V to look down to check the spelling of the name on the discipline file to take the opportunity to swiftly kick Dolby in the nearest shin. He winced, yelped and quickly looked out the window to his right so Steele would not get the satisfaction of seeing teardrops fall from his eyes. An early October storm brewed outside and the swirling red and orange leaves scraping against the window matched the chaos in Dolby's head and life. The howling wind wasn't helping matters for Dolby, either. He had always had a fear and hatred of windstorms ever since he could remember, due to a few scary moments in his past. And in his most honest moments, he had to admit that he had also developed a hatred for whoever was behind those winds. If those winds were the result of someone's work, he wanted nothing to do with him, or her, or it. Combined with the fear of Steele, Dolby felt as if he could be sick.

Thankfully, the absent-minded principal forgot the line of questioning aimed at Dolby and turned his attention now to Steele. Mr. V took a loud swig from his coffee mug and wearily sighed under his breath, "And what are we going to do with you, son?" Shaking his head, and with a shaking hand to match, he began flipping through Steele's folder. "We have had this discussion before, young man. It says here the last incident involving you was back in late September when you hung this same young man up by his overalls on a towel hook in the locker room." Dolby was furious. The old man had forgotten that incident already? He sure hadn't. It had been such a humiliating experience that he vowed that night never to wear the overalls again, even though they had been his favorite thing in all the world to wear. Little did he know that he would one day put them on again.

"You are on my last nerve and nearing the last straw. Do you want to be expelled? Because it sure seems like it to me." Steele lowered his head pretending to care. Mr. Vanderflunder rose from his desk, turned around and began to adjust a diploma on the wall. With an exhausted exhale, he announced to anyone that cared to hear, "I went into education forty-five years ago to make a difference in the lives of kids, and all I end up doing is dealing with problems." As if on cue, Steele reached around with his right hand and smacked Dolby in the back of the head. Dolby knew speaking up wouldn't do any good. Steele would simply deny any wrongdoing and make things worse with increased wrath. So, Dolby moved his chair as far away from the bully as he could, but unfortunately it meant drawing closer to the wind and the rains that he hated so much. He secretly fantasized that someone was outside the window witnessing it all and would intervene on his behalf. If anybody had only been outside, they would have seen very clearly the abuse being heaped upon Dolby from the hand, foot, mouth, and face of Steele Canis.

And then suddenly . . . CRASH!!! The shattering of glass interrupted his daydreaming! Like a scene from a cartoon, Mr. Vanderflunder had for-gotten the coffee cup in his hand, and while using both hands to straighten a picture, dumped hot coffee all over himself. His arm sprang upward in pain, catching the corner of the picture, knocking it off of the wall. On its way down, it found the corner of the desk, and exploded splintered pieces all over the office. Steele impulsively laughed and without thinking, mockingly announced, "Mr. V pulled a vanderflunder! He vanderflundered it!" The absent-minded principal had such a history and reputation at the school for his forgetfulness and clumsiness that his last name had been turned into a word that described when anyone messed up. This of course was thanks to a certain eighth grader who had a gift for such things.

Dolby immediately began to help Mr. V clean up the shards of glass, first placing the biggest fragments in the trash can and then brushing smaller bits from the desk onto the carpet to vacuum later. Of course, Steele remained in his chair, enjoying the scene so thoroughly that the only thing missing was a bucket of popcorn. When the dust settled, Dolby himself settled into his chair to the right of Steele, bracing for what was to come next. Little did he know that what he braced for was to be far more stag-gering and life-changing than simply receiving a scolding from a scalding principal.

2

ATTACK

"A wounded deer leaps the highest."
—*EMILY DICKINSON (1860)*

The aged principal shuffled slowly toward the window in dramatic silence in what seemed like an attempt to gather his thoughts for the upcoming verbal storm. In reality, he was oddly drawn to the thunderstorm outside that grew louder and more threatening by the second and began to think about their safety. Dolby faced the floor, awaiting his fate with his chin down, braced by his right hand. His right elbow rested on his right knee when he began to feel a wet sensation dripping down his arm. Bright red, sticky blood from a glass cut trickled from the back of his wrist down his arm and dripped onto the carpet below. Almost as if the discovery of blood angered the outside forces even further, the wind beat against the school window with more force. Dolby wiped the blood with his t-shirt, trying to ignore the noise. For some reason, he thought at that moment of his imaginary witness who might see the blood through the window, conclude that Steele was to blame, and somehow exact vengeance for him. When one has no friends, even imaginary ones can be comforting. All at once, though, branches were hurled in their direction and slammed against the pane, causing everyone to jump. Mr. Vanderflunder heeded the warning and waddled away as quickly as he could. Dolby, too, was sent scrambling across the room, his mind also being sent scrambling back to the trauma of a previous windstorm. Steele, however, had turned his chair toward the outdoors either in an act of stupidity or defiance, as if he had to prove to the world that he wasn't scared. Whether he was afraid or not, he was nonetheless about to receive the fright of his young life.

Even though the thunder was louder and nearer than ever, and the thunderbolts were lighting up the dark sky and room, it became clear that there was more than just a storm raging outside. At the exact moment of a lightning strike just yards away from the building, a thunderous BOOM exploded in everyone's ears. The lights in the room flickered and then faded out altogether, as the entire building lost power. Only it wasn't the boom of thunder—it was the familiar sound of glass shattering once more. They impulsively shielded their faces. When they dared to peek through their fingers and hands, they couldn't believe what they were seeing. As if right out of a horror movie, just ten feet away, twelve points of a buck's antlers were ripping and shredding through glass, wood, brick, and drywall like a chainsaw in the hands of a madman. The monster made quick work of the window and wall and with one giant leap, shook the room with a landing that was bent on vengeance. From Steele's viewpoint, lightning flashed behind the beast revealing the silhouette of a deer the size of a Grizzly Bear. Steele screamed like a girl as the savage walked methodically toward him, as if to heighten the torture. As Steele stood up from the chair, the muscular creature lowered and twisted his head. With the points of the right side of his rack, it gently prodded the boy in the chest, forcing him to slowly back up against the wall. Besides its black nose and eyes, it was thick with black fur on top of its head, between its eyes, and surrounding its mouth and nose, giving him the look of a bearded devil. Even though a deer, he was actually closer in size to an elk or moose. Twisting his head once again, the spiky horns now simultaneously dug into the wall, trapping the bully. It created what looked like a rib cage surrounding a heart, with the heart being the head of a helpless Steele, whose heartbeat itself raced in terror. He could feel the heat of the beast's breath, and he gagged at the musty smell. He was too paralyzed with fear to scream. A growing circle of wetness appeared on his jeans, but it wasn't from the rain. The buck stopped moving and all Steele could hear was the rhythmic grunting of the animal, his own heartbeat, and the periodic claps of thunder. Suddenly, the snorting grew louder and more intense as if the brute was trying to communicate some kind of threat but was frustrated by the language barrier. Stringy, wet discharge from the horned creature's mouth and nostrils showered Steele's face. The increasing mania of the monster resulted in increased terror. Steele screamed, "HELP! DO SOMETHING, DOUGH-BOY! HELP ME, DOUGH-BOY!" So complete was Steele's bullying of Dolby that even in a crisis, abuse was his natural default. Almost as if it could understand his words, a new singular frenzy possessed the animal the instant the insult flew from Steele's lips. At that moment, a new power forced the antlers deeper into the dry wall and closer and closer to the face of the panic-stricken boy. Steele turned his head inside the cage while there was still time, fully expecting the worst. Just then, two simple words thundered and reverberated throughout the darkness. "NO! STOP!"

Steele later remembered wondering at that moment whose voice it was that echoed through the room. It couldn't have been the old man, who by this time had fainted in a heap in the corner. And it surely couldn't have been the high-pitched voice of his weakling rival. But it *had* been the voice of Dolby. And the force and authority with which it was broadcasted surprised even Dolby himself. What had come over him was something completely foreign. It was not only a feeling of utter confidence, but also a powerful wave of command. For a brief moment, he was not afraid or insecure or uncertain. He was calmly in control in a way that felt . . . well, right. His two-word demand for obedience instantly stopped the deer's rage and forward momentum. The buck's eyes were instantly broken of its madness and now looked toward Dolby with submission. The antlers now began working their way slowly from the hold of the wall, and it backed away from the boy, still looking at Dolby out of the corner of its eyes. With the cage removed, Steele collapsed to the floor sobbing in relief. The 400-pound monster now advanced toward Dolby, who was strangely not afraid. Dolby instead smiled with approval as if he were a family pet. The newly tamed buck approached the boy with its head down in a posture of complete obedience. It then did something surprising that stirred in Dolby another new feeling of purpose he had never felt before. The twelve-pointed massive creature bent his right leg, lowered his black forehead, and bowed in honor before the youth. Without thinking, Dolby reached out his hand and placed it upon the black fur between the antlers as if with favor and appreciation. The deer raised its head, their eyes met, Dolby smiled, and like a flash of lightning, it bounded out of what used to be a window and into the thick forest just outside of the school.

At that moment, Dolby strangely noticed three things. First, the storm had died down completely. The second thing he observed was a black tail bouncing away into the forest. Because deer had always been his absolute favorite animal, he had grown into something of an expert. He knew that black-tailed deer were not native to central Michigan, where he lived. He remembered that there were two different black-tailed deer species, all of which lived in parts far away like Canada, Alaska, and the Pacific states of California, Oregon, and Washington. He wondered why a black-tailed buck had come all of this way to his little hometown.

By this time, Steele, still slumped down on the ground, had recovered enough to fix his confused gaze on his nemesis. "How did you do that?" he pressed, emphasizing each word.

"Do what?" came the reply.

"How did you talk with that animal?" Dolby paused because he really had no answer.

"I . . . I don't know. I just yelled at him to stop and I guess that was enough?" Steele's eyes squinted with suspicion.

"NO! You *GRUNTED!* You grunted and snorted at him in the exact same way that he had grunted and snorted at me." Dolby now looked as confused as the bully.

"I . . . um . . . I don't know what you mean. I literally yelled 'no' and 'stop,' and that's it." Dolby rehearsed the incident in his mind. He *had* spoken English, *hadn't* he?

Steele shook his head with further skepticism, "I know what I heard. And you grunted something in his direction, and he immediately understood." Dolby shrugged his shoulders not knowing what to say to that. Steele continued looking at him like he was some kind of a freak, and the familiar surge of feeling like a freak returned to Dolby. Steele got up, violently dusted himself off, and before exiting the room angrily pointed at the sixth grader, "Something is very weird here, Dough-boy. I'm going to be watching you." At that moment, it hadn't occurred to Steele that Dolby had probably saved his life.

The third thing Dolby observed as the buck leaped away? He had seen him before. He had definitely seen him before.

Mrs. Krantz may have been slow of foot, but she was the first of many school officials to pour in to assess the damage. As Mr. Vanderflunder came-to, Dolby suddenly remembered the embarrassing message he had left on the library computer. In a renewed panic, he ducked out and sprinted down the hall to the library. He fully intended to delete the message, until, with a wiggle of the mouse, the screen went from black to horrifying. The pounding of Dolby's heartbeat matched the blinking of the cursor. Somebody had been there. Immediately below the words, "Nobody likes me" was the following:

```
me 2. i know how u feel
```

3

WALK

"A light wind swept over the corn, and all nature laughed in the sunshine."
—*Anne Bronte in The Tenant of Wildfell Hall (1848)*

Dolby took advantage of the ongoing chaos from the attack, loaded up his backpack and snuck out of a side door, knowing nobody would miss him. He lived close enough to the school to walk home. But, then again, everyone lived close enough to walk home in Gomer. His head was swimming from what had just happened. Had he really stopped that buck from hurting Steele? He had acted without thinking, and yet the animal obviously responded to him. He knew that if he had time to think about it, he wouldn't have stopped anything. It would have been his turn to sit back, eat some popcorn, and enjoy the show.

The storm was now past as he made his way down a back-country road toward his house. He was halfway there when he felt that familiar sense of being watched. To his left, at a distant end of a corn field, stood seven deer who all lifted up their heads from grazing at the same time. They stared at him without moving as if in the proverbial headlights. Dolby's mind instantly flashed back to the last time deer were lining up to gawk at him. It was on a similar walk home, but the day had been far worse. It was after his first day at Gomer Middle School. He was already feeling upset that he had to move to a new school. He was also feeling out of place, alone, and anxious. Unfortunately, in those types of situations, his stomach would join him in feeling upset. It wasn't uncommon for Dolby to so work himself up during new and strange life events, that his lunch would also work its way up. For most kids, standing up in front of the class to share a little bit about oneself was a piece of cake. But Dolby is not like most kids. When Miss Daken innocently asked him to the front of the class, he came forward hoping it would be different this time. It wasn't. Instead, his stomach had a story to tell, and apparently it was a comedy because the entire class ended up erupting in laughter.

After being whispered about and laughed at for the rest of the afternoon, he made the trip home in complete humiliation. It took just one day of school for him to be shunned. So, when a group of young does began to stupidly look him over, he completely flipped out. It felt like they were mocking him, too. He proceeded to take out his pain on them. "STOP LOOKING AT ME!" he screamed. "THE FREAK SHOW IS OVER!" He then lost even more control and sprinted toward them, violently waving his arms. "GO AWAY! LEAVE ME ALONE!" The gentle creatures continued to stare, but now with a much more confused look. Then, he heard a loud noise above his shouts. An antlered monster raised its giant head and breast, snorted with such force that the other deer heeded the warning and took off into the woods. The buck raised and lowered its head and rack, repeatedly stomped its front hoof on the ground, and continued to snort in Dolby's direction. Frightened out of his funk, Dolby took the hint. If he had a tail, it would've been between his legs as he escaped back to the road. The last thing he remembered as he looked back over his shoulder was the unique black markings on the face and tail of the beast.

He was used to the presence of deer in his life. Ever since he could remember, they were his favorite animal. Oddly, he started to realize that he seemed to be their favorite animal as well. He began to question whether his experience with the deer species was different than the experiences of others. Maybe he should have figured it out earlier in life since his parents *had* nicknamed him "The Deer Whisperer" growing up. On every long-distance car trip that he could remember, he had the uncanny ability to spot deer in nearby fields before either of his parents. In fact, it became a family game to see if anyone could detect deer on the horizon before Dolby. Of course, they never could. He loved feeling the pride that came from discovering them first, even if only from the backseat of the car. When it came to deer, his father was vigilant in making sure that each of the family vehicles were outfitted with deer whistles. Wind from the moving car rushed through the mounted plastic devices on the front grill to create a high-pitched sound that only deer could hear. This caused deer to not only take notice, but also to run away in order to avoid both the sound, and an animal-to-car collision. Dolby remembered the effectiveness of those whistles. But, after reexamining things in light of recent events, he also now wondered if it was more than the deer whistles that was getting their attention. Could it be that deer were somehow and for some reason also interested in him? Lost in thoughts such as these, he was then awakened by another unusual scene. He had approached a stretch of road that was sandwiched on both sides by more open fields, lined by trees of red, orange and yellow. He became aware that there was significant amount of movement on both sides of him. As he walked along, young fawns, who were still spotted from their birth three months before, were playing and dancing together. The sun's rays poked through the clouds creating multiple spotlights shining on the dozens of playing and dancing fawns. They played and danced along with Dolby as he walked. Playing and dancing surrounded him! It was hard for Dolby not to conclude that they were doing so in celebration of him! Was he imagining it? Was he just daydreaming something that he wished to be true? Did he want to be accepted by kids his own age so badly that his mind was playing tricks on him? High-pitched bleating from the young deer interrupted these questions. Dolby knew that fawns only bleated like baby goats when they were threatened or injured. But, despite what he had always known, there was no mistaking the sound he was hearing. It was pure freedom, fun, and happiness. In light of how poorly he was used to being treated, it was both too good to be true, and too much for him to take in. He started to run. As he scampered away, he didn't quite notice the presence of a soft, cool breeze at his back nudging him home. All he knew at that moment was what he needed to do next.

4

JOURNALS

"A tree house, a free house, A secret you and me house,
A high up in the leafy branches, cozy as can be house.
A street house, a neat house, be sure to wipe your feet house
Is not my kind of house at all—Let's go live in a tree house."

—*SHEL SILVERSTEIN IN WHERE THE SIDEWALK ENDS (1974)*

The rickety, screen door of the old farmhouse slammed shut three times as Dolby tried to catch his breath inside. He was thankful that his Grandma was not at home—he didn't have to make something up about why he was home early from school. He raced up the staircase to his room. Shutting the door and locking it, he pulled back a corner of the carpet behind the door, revealing wooden planks of floorboard. With a flat-head screwdriver, he pried up a loose plank. Under the flooring was just enough room for a twelve-year old's valuables, which included six different-sized notebooks. He lifted them up, replaced the board and carpet, and sat down to reread memories that he hadn't laid eyes on since they had been penned.

Dolby had kept journals off and on since he was in second grade. They started out as letters to imaginary friends—the only friends that he wasn't socially awkward around. By telling them his thoughts, it made him feel as if he wasn't quite so alone. Later notebooks were filled with entries at the encouragement of counselors who wanted him to get more in touch with his feelings. Either way, the diary entries served as windows into the past that might offer clues to what was going on. Besides, he had completely forgotten events from his earliest diaries. He spent the next few hours holed up in his room pouring over journals filled with drawings, letters, and the retelling of stories that sounded more like fiction than reality. Anyone else reading over them would have probably marveled at Dolby's highly-developed imagination at such a young age. But as he read account after account, he knew they were real. He had lived through them. He was just now realizing how truly unique his experiences were. Dolby dog-eared corners of pages that were especially intriguing to revisit later. He stuffed them in his book bag, plopped down on his bed and tried to make sense of it all. Unable to focus, he went downstairs, devoured two peanut butter and jelly sandwiches, wrestled on his backpack again and headed out the back door to what had become his favorite place on earth.

He discovered it on one of the many times he went exploring since arriving at his grandmother's house. She lived on five acres that once served as a boarding farm for horses. But, behind her property were hundreds more acres of woods that were the perfect playground for a boy who preferred animals to people and being alone to crowds. The truth is, he hadn't really discovered it at all, as he originally thought at the time. Looking back, he now sees that it was shown to him. It was a Sunday night in late August, he had just moved in with his grandma the week before, and he was dreading his first day of school the next day. Dolby was beyond the barn setting up fireworks to shoot off in an empty, fenced-in pasture. Fireworks were a favorite pastime of Dolby's. It was one of the few times that he felt powerful and in control of his life. He was just about to send up a bottle rocket when he heard rustling in the tall grass past the fence. The rustling got louder, which aroused his curiosity. He cautiously approached the dry, brown meadow but could not see what was making the noise. He could only see the tall vegetation move as the creature slowly walked away. He caught glimpses of a small, spotted animal about the size of a large dog. The fawn led Dolby through the tall grass, looking back every once in a while to make sure she was still being followed. She came to a clearing where she bounced and skipped from one place of cover to another. Each time a new hiding spot was found, she looked back to check the status of her companion. Dolby was as fascinated by this graceful wildlife creature as ever and felt that he was being drawn by her like a magnet. They crossed over Cedar Creek. She led him for a few minutes through some thick woodlands, until the forest opened up into two large fields that were separated by a center strip of trees, thick with leaves that were just starting to turn colors. But, he had lost her. He scanned the field on his right. He then walked through the thin strip of foliage to the field on the left. But there was no sign of his new friend. He thought maybe she walked through the line of trees in front of him, so he began to make his way through the undergrowth. After about a hundred yards, he still hadn't caught wind of her. But he did find something else. A large oak tree stood in the middle of the tree line and attached to its trunk was a fifteen-foot tall ladder leading up to the coolest tree stand he had ever seen. He climbed the planks of the ladder which led him to an open wooden deck that extended out on top of a large limb. There was another five feet of rungs that he excitedly scaled that led to a door to an enclosed stand that, due to its size, was more like a tree house than a blind. He could see for what seemed like miles out of four horizontal rectangular openings that looked out in all four directions, no doubt for a hunter to shoot from. His first thought as he peered out of his new home away from home? Maybe this is going to work out after all. His second thought? This would be perfect if it didn't keep swaying in the breeze.

Since that discovery, Dolby added many personal touches to the abandoned hunter's roost. There was now a beanbag chair, an area rug, a battery-powered radio, a pile of comic books stacked on a table made from a stump, a flashlight, a pair of binoculars, and a chest full of fireworks that his grandma threatened to throw out if he continued to keep them at the house. Removing his backpack, he sank down into the beanbag chair and began to reread the marked journal pages. The first dog-eared sheet was from second grade and contained a memory he had completely forgotten. Written in the chicken scratch of an earlier version of himself was the following:

> I had fun tuday. Mom and Dad me to the zoo. My favrite was the petting zoo. Wen i gav milk to a baby cow, all the baby deer wanted it. Thar wur 8 and thay licked me ovr and ovr. Tha woodnt leaf me alone. Lik i was thayr mom or sumting.

An entry dated two years later said,

> You will never gess what happened. I was catchin fireflies in the backyard tonite when I saw a doe laying down under a tree. I moved close to it and it didn't run away. I moved slowly so if wouldn't get scarred. It just stayed under the tree. I got close and it let me touch it. I petted it and talked to it like it was my dog!"

Another entry from the fifth grade recalled,

> *It happened again today. On the bus ride home, Jimmy threw his lunch box at me. It hit me in the back and it really hurt. I was crying when I got off the bus and then I saw a deer right by my house. It seems like every time something bad happens to me, a deer appears almost like it feels bad and wants to help me. Or like it knows. Deer are kinda becoming like friends.*

There were many more like that. All of these journal entries were reminders that he had always had unusual encounters with deer growing up. He now realized that they were normal only to him. But, ever since his move to Gomer, those "chance" meetings had increased both in number, and in the wonder, they produced. Ironically, with that thought, Dolby began to hear the surrounding woodlands come alive with strange noises he had not heard in person before. Quietly at first, sounds echoed from every direction that didn't seem to belong together. There was ear-piercing, high-pitched trumpeting that morphed into pig-like squealing. There was a deep mooing that mixed with intense grunting like a bear. There was even a low growl that resembled that of a lion. All of these sounds together transformed the nearby forest into what seemed like the music of a weird jungle. He grabbed the binoculars but could not locate the sources of any of the cries; they were too distant and buried too deeply into the woods. Even so, thanks to YouTube, he did not need to see what was making all of the racket. He knew. But, he didn't know how it was possible. Why were different male species of Elk, Caribou, Moose, Red Deer and Mule Deer traveling from some of the farthest corners of the North American continent to gather in little Gomer, Michigan? Why had he seen a black-tailed buck from all the way across the country? What in the world was going on? He was overcome with a sinking feeling that he was about to play a role it. Even though he had always wanted to make a difference and to be somebody, now he wasn't so sure.

Somehow, he also caught another faint sound from off in the distance. This one was the ringing of an outdoor cast iron dinner bell from his grandmother.

The computer messages continued back and forth. There was at least one per day. On some days, multiple notes filled the desktop screen. Dolby was careful to visit the computer early in the morning before most everyone arrived, during lunch when the library was empty, and any other chance he got when he could be alone in front of the blinking cursor.

```
                                              nobody likes me


me 2. i know how u feel


                                              who is this


a friend


                                    i don't have any friends


me neither
```

5

DISCOVERY

"But I like the animals better than the 'best people.'"

—*HUGH LOFTING IN THE STORY OF DOCTOR DOOLITTLE (1920)*

Dolby reflected on the school day as he walked home. It hadn't been a bad day, but he was still feeling sad nonetheless. Steele Canis had thankfully backed off after the incident in Mr. Vanderflunder's office. But in some ways, the damage was done. Everyone in the entire school was afraid of Steele, which meant that everyone was afraid to talk to Dolby. In fact, he heard the slur "Dough-boy" almost every day. Steele made it clear early on that a friend of Dolby's was an enemy of Steele's. Combined with Dolby's social clumsiness, he lamented the fact that despite a new start at a new school, there was little hope for anything new to happen in the friendship category. It was a little comforting to remember that at least he had a new computer pal.

He walked straight to the treehouse, which was now his normal practice after school. It had become a place of refuge and safety, and he found a strange sense of belonging there that he didn't find anywhere else. It was hard to feel sorry for himself to the soundtrack of birds singing, leaves blowing, and the rushing water of the nearby creek. At the very least, he was able to focus on homework better. He popped open a bag of Doritos left over from lunch, took a sip from his water bottle, and cracked open a social studies textbook.

It was also his normal practice in such a peaceful place to nod off in his beanbag chair while studying. Today was no different. What was different, however, was that he awoke not to the hammering of a woodpecker or the scurrying of a squirrel or rabbit below. Almost as unexpected as the bellowing of Moose and Elk the week before, Dolby was stirred from his nap by the distinct cries of a child. Still in a fog, he scrambled down the ladder in the direction of the muffled sobs. He had a hard time tracking the youngster because he or she would be whining one minute, and then silent the next. At one point, he thought he heard a high-pitched "help!" He wondered what a child was doing so deep in the woods. He continued stumbling through thick brush in an attempt to locate the source of the struggle but decided that he must be going in circles. Tired and sweaty from being out of shape, Dolby was tempted to just go back and get help. But, then a twig snapped loudly. Something large rustled in the thicket. A good-sized whitetail doe emerged from the brambles with a look of desperation. She squinted and pleaded with her eyes at the sound of squealing in the distance. "HELP!" He heard it this time for sure. It was high and immature and pierced through the woods. The doe's white tail popped up as she ran. Dolby followed her. She led him to a small hillside where Dolby had to grab thin seedlings to help ascend the slope. The cries were louder and closer and just over the ridge. When he got to the top, he stopped in his tracks, and not just because he was exhausted. There, beside the anxious doe, was a small, spotted fawn caught in an old, barbed-wire fence. Dolby quizzically looked around for the child. The mother skipped in place and wheezed to get back Dolby's attention. The fawn did the same, painfully bleating loudly like a baby goat. Dolby stared in confusion. The baby deer definitely just shrieked, "PLEEEEEAAAAAASE!"

Dolby set that aside in his head as he went to work. It wriggled and struggled, making it harder for Dolby to free it from the metal barbs. He methodically pulled and twisted and shoved and pried both fence and fawn and soon had the baby freed from the grasp of the fence's hold. The mother rushed over and instantly began to lick the wounds of her baby. As she did, the fawn herself began to lick Dolby up and down his arms and hands. Dolby recoiled, both hands shooting up in the air as if at gunpoint. His face betrayed the fact that he was questioning his own sanity. His accusation even sounded crazy. "Were you yelling 'help?'" The spotted creature continued licking. "DID YOU YELL, 'PLEASE?'" . . . nothing. He turned to the doe. "DID YOUR BABY SPEAK?!" Perhaps he raised his voice too much, but it got the mother's attention. She stopped attending to the lacerations, raised her head and with what seemed like a smile, made a sneezing sound out of her nose. The doe then nuzzled Dolby's hand with her wet nose as if with gratitude. She prodded the youngster in its side, and mother and child gracefully bounced away. "WAIT!" Dolby shouted. "AM I GOING CRAZY?!" They ignored him. "HEY!" Dolby pleaded. At that, the female stopped, looked at Dolby, nodded her head toward a blackberry patch to his right and snorted once more.

Dolby turned his head in time to see, emerging from the bushes, the same giant black-tailed stag carrying twelve points on its black head, and an oval ring around its nose and mouth. Instinctively, Dolby backed away and bowed his head before the impressive specimen that he had met before. The buck opened his mouth, but what came out was a guttural grunt that sounded like the word "NO." More low groans followed, but Dolby couldn't make out if they were supposed to be words. Sensing this, the beast groaned even lower and slower. It took him some time, but Dolby began to decipher some of the words. He was conscious of having to retrain his ears and mind. Soon, phrases began to surface. "Blacktail give honor. No honor to black-tail." He heard it!

With excitement, Dolby blurted, "Is that your name? Are you Blacktail?"

The beast paused. "No. I belong to the black-tailed. They are my kind. The blacktail call me Shadow Muzzle." Dolby looked his nose over.

"What do the no-tail call you?" Dolby also paused. No-Tail? "When whitetail speak of your kind, we say no-tail."

"Ohhhh," he answered, "I am Dolby." Shadow Muzzle's right knee lowered to the ground.

"Shadow Muzzle give honor." Dolby couldn't contain himself and began spitting out question after question.

"How can I understand you?

How can you understand me?

Why are you here?

Why did I hear moose and elk?

Why did you break through the school?

Why am I seeing more deer than ever?

What does this . . ."

"ENOUGH," came the roar. "There will be time for questions. Now not time. Follow Shadow." Dolby kept his eyes on the black-dipped tail as it led him in silence over rocks, through briers, and under pine branches. They marched on for the better part of an hour. The route on which Shadow Muzzle led him was so curvy and confusing that Dolby figured it was an attempt to keep their destination hidden. They eventually found a path that wound its way up a small summit. The path was well-worn and tree-lined. Like thirty-foot tall soldiers welcoming royalty, the thin evergreens stood rapt at attention as if either someone of great importance was passing by, or something of great significance was about to happen; or both. It was a miniature hill compared to what the black-tailed deer was used to back home, but it was large by Michigan's standards. Shadow Muzzle ascended the hill with ease and led Dolby right to a dead end of more pine trees. The buck made a careful search and smell of his surroundings. Satisfied that they were alone, he then stomped a complicated cadence on the ground. A muffled snort that Dolby couldn't make out responded. The black-tail snorted back a message that he understood to be, "Half-tail." Two large racks of antlers appeared through the pine needles and an opening was slowly created as if curtains were being pulled back. Dolby's eyes got as big as if he were a star on a stage. There was no spotlight. But, he stood there unable to move, paralyzed at the sight, as if battling stage fright.

6

WISDOM

"And one year it fell out that Tumnus came down river and brought them news
that the White Stag had once more appeared in his parts
—the White Stag who would give you wishes if you caught him."

—C.S. LEWIS IN
THE LION, THE WITCH AND THE WARDROBE (1950)

The thicket opened up to reveal a scene that Dolby couldn't have made up. On the top of the hill, Dolby estimated dozens of acres extending out before him. Some of it more wooded than others, but all of it filled with a flurry of activity. Hundreds of deer of varying types were bustling around, busy with purpose. In the brief time he had to take it all in, he saw a group of moose taking turns head-butting a fallen log. He saw elk wallowing together in a muddy swamp in an organized fashion. There were white-tailed bucks paired up and clanging antlers together as if in the middle of some kind of sparring practice. Other male blacktails were sharpening their points on a tree. There were plenty of does feeding and preparing beds, while fawns played at their feet. In some ways, it reminded him of a military camp preparing for battle.

He felt nudges on his back as two female red deer, appearing out of nowhere, forced him forward through a pathway surrounded on both sides by pine branches. The opening shut behind him. As he made his way through the hallway of fir trees, he heard the unmistakable trumpeting of a male elk. It seemed the entire camp answered with movement. In a matter of seconds, various animals were lined up in front of Shadow Muzzle and Dolby, creating a path to walk through. Mature males with great racks of antlers made up the parade route. They all stood at attention with heads lowered and horns touching, forming an arch under which Dolby was clearly supposed to walk. He was in awe of the various sizes and species and colors of the different beasts as he traveled easily under the spiky tunnel. There were dozens of mule deer, moose, elk, black-tailed and white-tailed deer, and even Caribou. Though he felt undeserving of such a welcome, he also noticed a strange wave of confidence surging through him. He eyeballed Shadow with a puzzled look. Knowingly, he thundered, "We are here to see Fantasma," as if that meant anything to Dolby. His continued look of confusion surprised the buck. He sighed. "Oh. I am blacktail. My father was mule deer. We not known for wisdom. I here for strength, as are many of these. Fantasma here for wisdom. She answer questions." The lineup led to the edge of a bluff, where a smaller hill loomed in front of them. They climbed another gravel path until they arrived at a clearing fenced in by thick brush. They were at the very top of the summit. To the right was an opening that overlooked miles and miles of rivers and woodlands. Shadow motioned toward a flat boulder. Dolby sat down, panting as he admired the view. Shadow also laid down next to him. As far as the eye could see were hills and woods topped with gorgeous October reds, yellows, oranges and purples. They sat in silence, and Dolby waited patiently for what was next. He couldn't help but notice a pleasant breeze swirling about them bringing sweet smells from nearby wildflowers, and he was content. He could've sat there all night.

Lost in wonder, he lost track of the time when Shadow Muzzle quickly stood up at the sound of footsteps. Dolby followed suit. He jerked his head back in time to witness two enormous light-gray caribou surface from a grove of birch trees. Behind them gracefully tiptoed the most beautiful and mysterious creature he had ever seen. Though she was half the size of the blacktail, her noble manner made her seem bigger. She glided over and nodded elegantly at Shadow, who nodded back and uttered, "Fantasma!"

She lowered her head, smiled and blinked her eyes. Turning next to Dolby, a soft, soothing voice announced, "Greetings, Half-tail!" Dolby was mesmerized. She was a white-tailed doe whose skin and fur were completely milky white in color so that she almost glowed against the dark green backdrop. Her eyes, nose, and inside of her ears were light pink. Otherwise, she appeared to be bleached from head to hoof. Even her hooves were an almost white light-gray. Dolby had heard of albino deer, and had seen pictures, but never thought he'd see one in person.

Not knowing what to say, he awkwardly blurted out, "Why do you call me half-tail?"

She shifted her weight and chuckled. "Have a seat. There are many questions to be answered."

7

WINDMASTER

"All I know is that I grew up not questioning God because that's how we were. God was there like the birds and the wind."

—*Jane Goodall*

Fantasma laid down next to the rock, making Dolby feel at ease. She motioned to the caribou to leave them alone, making him feel even more at ease. "I am sure you have noticed by now that there is something very special about you that we only see once in a generation or more. You are what we call a 'half-tail.' Even though you are a no-tail by birth, you have been given a special ability to understand and speak the tongue of the whitetail, and others like us. You are not fully a member of the tail kingdom, but as one who can speak both tongues, we consider you half-tail. That is why you no doubt have noticed that you are a curiosity to our kind."

"But how is that possible? I have always been a nobody to the no-tail." He surprised even himself to hear the lingo being picked up so quickly.

"That is where you err. Each creature, no matter the kind, is unique and special in its own way, whether aware of it or not. Each one has been gifted with special purposes." The wheels were clearly turning in Dolby's brain, though he had a hard time buying what he was hearing.

"You don't understand. I am—and I have always been—a loser. A freak. A failure." Fantasma nodded knowingly.

"Do you forget already who it is that you talk to? I am a freak to my kind. I am named 'Fantasma Bianca,' which in some of the tongues of the no-tail means 'Ghost' or 'Phantom of the Wood.' Every time I hear my name, I am reminded of my abnormalities. Every time I see my reflection in a creek, I see a freak of nature staring back at me. I am anything but normal and yet, that didn't stop gifts of wisdom to be given me beyond my kind."

Somehow, Dolby knew the statistic. "You are definitely unique. I think there is one albino per 30,000 Whitetail."

"Again, you are mistaken. I am one in more than a million, because there is none created exactly like me. I am unique among the albino too. Remember, friend, *it is the same with you.*" Dolby was uncomfortable both with thinking of himself that way, and with considering the idea of a Creator.

He changed the subject. "I have so many questions. How is it that I can understand you? How do you understand me? Why are you here in Gomer? Why are so many animals gathering from far away?"

She turned into a wise, old guru, and answered, "Every question you ask, and yes, every question that could possibly be asked, has one answer. The answer to all is 'the Windmaster.'" Dolby tried to keep up. "Our paths have been blown together by the Master of the Wind." At that, Dolby cringed with anger, remembering his past. "We understand each other because the Windmaster has blown His favor in our direction, a mysterious swirling together of the winds."

"Okaaaaay." Dolby was perplexed. "But why are we all gathering right now in Gomer? What exactly is going on?"

"We do not yet know. Even I do not yet know. It has not been made known to us. We have been driven here by the wind and are awaiting the next breeze. All we know is that something is brewing on the horizon that requires our service. So, we prepare ourselves. Dolby?"

"Yes?"

"It is very important that this gift of yours remain a secret kept between you, the whitetail and the Windmaster. You are *not* to tell anyone about your secret skill. It could put our kind in too much danger. Do you understand?" Dolby took a deep breath, afraid to ask his next question. He didn't need to. "I sense that you are suspicious of the Windmaster."

He struggled to find the words, but soon anger fueled them and they came fast and furious. "If there is such a thing, then He has only blown storms my way. Maybe I don't want to accept that a Windmaster exists because then I would have to conclude that He hates me." Dolby felt the surge of tears welling up in his eyes and quickly turned the questioning around. "What makes *you* think such a Windmaster exists?" Fantasma Bianco graciously laughed to herself as she got back on all fours. She began to walk around Dolby and the boulder like a lawyer making a closing argument.

"What you don't understand about our kind is that the wind is our lifeline. It carries the secret to our survival. It is through our noses that we smell dangers. We detect the aromas in the air to find food and water to stay alive. The wind currents lead us to new places of safety. We are steered to companions and mates by forces hidden in the wind. Without the winds, there are no whitetail or blacktail. We owe everything to the wind, and thus, to the Windmaker. You speak of damage that you've seen done by the wind. We both agree that even though we don't see the gale, we believe it exists because we see the results it leaves behind. For the whitetail, we do not see the Windmaster with our eyes. But, we clearly witness the things that He does for us; the results he leaves behind. We sense Him in the wind. We feel His guidance. We know His provision every day. Therefore, we don't think He exists. We *know* He does based on our experience. The difference between the no-tail and those in the tail kingdom is when we sense His presence, we listen, and we follow. And after following, we look back and see His hand at work. When the no-tail sense His presence, He is often doubted and questioned. You don't listen, you don't act, and you don't follow. And then you miss seeing the consequences that would have proved to you that He was there all along."

Dolby tried to process the conversation. Sensing this, the albino added, "It is getting dark, and you have a long walk ahead of you. There will be time for more questions later. I will send escorts with you to your house in the woods. I want you to think about one more thing on your journey." Dolby raised his eyebrows as if to say, "What?"

"When you first saw the treehouse, did you not wonder who built it? You don't ask *if* someone built it. You know for certain that at some point in time there was a builder. Learn from the whitetail. We live out-of-doors. We look at the trees and the rivers and the stars and we don't wonder *if* someone built the masterpiece before us. We *know* that He did."

Dolby stared at the latest message.

i don't have any friends

me neither
i could b ur friend
we could start texting

He didn't respond for days not knowing what to say. Part of him loved the idea of having somebody human to talk to, but the other part was skeptical. It could be somebody just messing with him again and having fun at his expense. But, man, did he want a real friendship. He was torn.

i don't have a cell phone or internet @ home.

can we keep talking this way?

but how do i know i can trust u?

8

PIGS

"The creatures outside looked from pig to man, and from man to pig to man again; but already it was impossible to say which was which."

—*GEORGE ORWELL IN ANIMAL FARM (1944)*

It may seem out of character for a kid who had spent his entire life feeling alone and out of place to change overnight and become confident in his own skin. Of course, he wasn't there yet. The reality of having to ignore insults and fend off bullies for as long as he was alive was still quite fresh in his mind. But, let's face it. In the course of just a couple of weeks, Dolby had discovered that he had a special power that nobody else had. He harnessed that power over a creature that was three times his size. He learned that his role was going to be essential in some yet unknown matter of great importance. Dolby secretly felt pretty darn good about himself. Too good, as it turned out.

He wasn't used to feeling so full of himself, but he liked it. One night after dinner, he went out to "play at a friend's." Instead, he hopped on his bike and peddled about two miles down the old gravel road to the nearest farm. He just had to investigate something. So as not to be seen, Dolby peeled off the main road early, and snuck down through the woods to get to the back of Farmer Brown's property. Proud of how quiet he was being, he frankly felt like he could do nothing wrong. That is, until the evening chorus of frogs and chirping crickets was joined by a herd of whitetail deer bedded down for the night in a nearby alfalfa field. Each one excitedly called out things like, "GOODNIGHT, HALF-TAIL! NICE NIGHT FOR A RIDE! SEE YOU TOMORROW AT THE TREEHOUSE? GOODNIGHT! SAY HI TO SHADOW FOR US!" He felt bad for shushing them, but he didn't want to have to face Farmer Brown. He never thought he'd see the day when talking with deer would become a nuisance!

He parked his bike outside of the barn and started his experiment first with the horses inside. He approached the first stall with a fresh apple in his hand. He held it out to a brown colt, who perked up and swallowed it whole. Dolby petted the white stripe down its nose and took a chance. "How do you like it here in Gomer?" His voice trailed off in an echo, sounding just as goofy as when it was first spoken aloud. "What does your kind call you?" The young steed whinnied with indifference, sniffing for another apple. He decided to try the whole barn, yelling. "Can anyone understand me?!" Feeling a little silly, but not enough to dampen his over-confidence in his new ability, he ventured outside to a fenced-in pig sty. "Hallo!" he shouted to the group of swine collecting in a corner. No response except for a few squeals. He tried a different approach. "Hello!" he shouted again. But this time he tried to vocalize the word with a much more oink-like tone from the back of his throat. He tried some different phrases like, "What did you eat for dinner?" and "Has the weather been cool enough for you?" Even Dolby had to chuckle at how ridiculous he sounded trying to pronounce words with a distinctively piggy sound. Not to be deterred, he remembered that his first real contact with understanding the deer language was with a young fawn. So, he crawled up to the fence where the piglets were to get down to their level. On all fours, in a high-pitched oink-like voice, Dolby grunted, "You guys are cute! Which one is your momma?" All of a sudden, he got that strange sensation of being watched again. But, this time it wasn't a deer that gawked. Dolby collapsed to the ground when he heard the voice behind him.

"Hey Sow-boy! Is that your new name?! What in thee heck are you doing, you ginger-haired Sow-boy?" Steele could hardly get it out of his mouth through the laughter. Steele had made good on his promise to keep his eyes on Dolby. He was out walking two of his dad's pit bulls, when he saw Dolby go off-roading on his bike. He followed half-expecting to catch Dolby doing something out of the ordinary, due to his recent sneaky behavior. But he didn't expect it to be *this* out of the ordinary. "Trough-boy? Is that any better? Get it, 'trough,' as in what pigs eat out of?!" Steele was enjoying himself way too much. He dragged the snarling pit bulls in Dolby's direction—or was it the other way around? Either way, Dolby was on all fours and cornered against a fence. As the dogs got closer, Dolby noticed old scars and new, bloody cuts all over the faces and paws of the two pit bulls, making them even scarier. "Where's your deer friend when you need him, huh?!"

Dolby had no choice. He had already been humiliated, and he didn't stand a chance against Steele and two dangerous attack dogs. It was his only option. He sat up, and with all of the breath he could muster, screamed, "HELP ME! SHADOW!" Steele paused and looked around cautiously, remembering the same grunting from the principal's office. After another low groan and another long silence, Steele moved in. He wasn't planning to really hurt Dolby. He just wanted to give a him little scare like Dolby had given him. Both barking dogs began whimpering like puppies at the shaking ground beneath their feet. Steele heard a stampede of hooves approaching from a distance. There was just enough light for Steele to make out at least twenty deer bolting his way. The dogs willingly obeyed as he yanked them in the opposite direction toward the road and to safety. The deer allowed the bully to leave, worrying more about Dolby. He softly cried, not knowing if it was more from fear or shame. His new friends surrounded him. "I'm sorry. I was thinking too highly of myself. I began to think that I was clever enough to speak with *any* animal. Shadow and Fantasma both made it clear that I was given a unique gift and was to use it wisely. If this ability is not for my enjoyment, then what is it meant for?" The herd was silent. The smallest deer of the bunch pushed forward, making her way to the front while mumbling something. Dolby really didn't expect an answer to the question. But the deer with the white spots mumbled a little louder. Dolby still couldn't make out what she said.

Finally, she got up the nerve to squeak skittishly, "Windmaster." Dolby braced himself, not really wanting to hear the rest. "The answer to every question is 'the Windmaster.' You asked what your power was meant for. The answer is for the Windmaster." Nothing else was spoken, for there was very little else to say.

One by one, the deer departed back to where they were bedded down, but not without a bow first. The last one to leave was the fawn who had just spoken, and sensing Dolby's inner turmoil, stumbled up to him. Dolby still sat on the ground at about the same height as the fawn. She threw her neck around his neck in an awkward, armless hug. She then started to skip away, when Dolby stopped her. "Wait! What do the whitetail call you?"

"I am named 'Snowflake,'" came the high-pitched answer. "We have met once before—at the barbed-wire fence. Remember?—you saved me!" She pranced away happily and joined the others.

Dolby sat rehashing the whole incident. He had seen Steele walk his pit bulls before. They lived in a small town, after all, and Steele lived relatively close to his grandma. What he hadn't noticed before was that these dogs were different than the ones Steele had walked in the past. And he had always seen them being walked from a distance. He wondered why both dogs had so many cuts on their faces? Had the other dogs sustained similar injuries?

but how do i know i can trust u?

4 starters, we can b sure r messages r only red by us
i wrote a password down on a piece of paper
& put it in ur locker
there is a file on this desktop called "tech backups"
open it up, use the password & u will see r thread
nobody will see r conversation
then delete this file

9

GEEMA

"When grace is joined to wrinkles, it is adorable.
There is something of the dawn in happy old age."

—*VICTOR HUGO IN LES MISERABLES (1845)*

The screen door in the back of the house rhythmically slammed four times in a row as Dolby barreled in from a forgettable day of school. His grandmother gasped at the harsh way the quiet farmhouse was so violently violated. He mumbled something as he sprinted through the kitchen toward the staircase, his voice trailing off up the stairs. The short, plump figure would have none of it. "DOLBY BRAD HART! SSSHHHTOPP! Get yourshelf back here young man!" Another short, plump figure stopped in his tracks and obeyed.

"Yes, ma'am."

"Isshh that anyway to greet your Geema?"

"No, ma'am." He went in for a hug but stopped short when he saw what sat on the counter. "GEEMA!"

"What?"

He pointed. "Oh, sharrr-rrrreeee," she sang. Slimy dentures were snapped up off of the counter and popped into her mouth like a handful of peanuts.

"Is that any way to greet your Geema?" she more clearly asked with arms outstretched, still smacking fake teeth into place. Dolby hugged her and thought she smelled more like old lady than ever. "What in tarnation is the emergency?"

"Oh . . . I . . . well,"—he wasn't very good at lying. "I was going to meet a new friend at the treehouse and forgot my slingshot." That part was true. "I promised Dell I'd meet him there." That part was not. Dolby was thinking of his computer buddy when trying to come up with a name. Dell was the first computer manufacturer that came to his mind. He was actually excited to play a new game he and Snowflake made up. He would gather acorns, lug them up to the landing of the blind and then sling them up into the air for his new fawn friend to catch and eat like candy. Others joined in of late since the foot of the Oak tree fort was always covered in acorns, and the top was always occupied by Dolby, an object of increased curiosity. He knew his Geema enough to know that his plans had just changed. She snipped green beans by the sink and without even a word, he now knew the reason why his plans had just changed. As he picked up a handful, he peered out of the kitchen window to see Snowflake nervously moving through the backyard bushes. Geema's underarm flab swayed to the rhythm of her bean snapping.

"How was your day at school?" (Pop . . . pop)

"Fine." (Pop . . . snip)

"Are you behaving yourself, young man?" (SNAP . . . SNAP) Was Dolby imagining it, or did she just snap the beans louder to make a point? She leaned in and glared at him over her glasses.

"Yes, Geema," he answered robotically. (Pop)

"Have you been in to see goofy ole' Mr. Vanderflunder lately?" (snip . . . snip)

"No, ma'am."

"Are you stayin' away from that Steele character?" (SNAP . . . SNAP . . . SNAP)

She wiped her hands on her apron, scowled at him and awaited the right answer. Her question was more of a demand than a question, and her voice was loud and firm. She popped the head off of the green bean in his direction as if it was his head!

Dolby understood and stammered, "Yes. He has left me alone lately, and I don't think I will have any more trouble from him for a while." How could such a sweet little old lady be equally as scary at the same time?

His grandmother resumed popping the ends off of the beans and started again in a sweet voice. "You know, I am not surprised he is a trouble-maker. The apple don't fall far from the tree with that one. His father was trouble ever since I can remember. In fact, he used to be known around Gomer as the town drunk. Still might be, far as I know. It got so bad that his wife left him years ago. Rumor has it that he lost his job and even became homeless. That's how he ended up in the old Dew Drop Inn Motel on the far end of town. The owner—Blarney was his name, I think—was losing money hand over fist and just up and moved to Wanesville and left it all behind. Ole' Swampy Canis swooped in—why *did* they call him 'Swampy' anyway?—and started living there as if he built it hisself. Nobody stopped him on account of feeling sorry for him. So, he just moved right in and has been livin' as a squatter there ever since . . . goin' on thirty years I s'pose. Not sure when Steele joined him and why. He's pretty private anymore, not really letting folks in on what he's up to. But, I have heard the police chief is always up there for something. Don't know if 'ole Swampy keeps gettin' into trouble, or if they's thick as thieves."

She was on a roll, and Dolby took advantage of it. "Have you heard anything about Swampy owning a bunch of pit bulls?"

"Oh sure. Years ago, there was talk that he was runnin' some kind of dog fighting ring up there. Reports come back that there's lotsa barking and traffic. Hard to say since it's all the way up Fowler's Hill and hidden away in the woods. Makes sense to me that all those motel rooms could be used for dog kennels. No one knows for sure, because unless you got business with Swampy or the police chief, you don't dare show your face up there."

"Really? Cause I saw a couple of his dogs up close, and they both had cuts and scars all over!"

"You what?! I thought I told you to stay away from that boy! He is nothing but trouble and . . ."

"Let me explain. I was behind Farmer Brown's house, when . . ."

"You what?!" she exclaimed. "What were you doing there? If I can't trust you, say goodbye to your precious treehouse."

"But, let me explain."

"You've said enough. You can explain it to the walls in your room until dinner time."

Dolby's shoulders sank as he slowly trudged upstairs. After watching her grandson ascend the stairs so pathetically, she felt a twinge of guilt for possibly overreacting. But, she reminded herself, she was all he had left. Who else was going to protect him? It was while thinking these things that she caught a glimpse through the window of Snowflake still playing patiently in the backyard. She all of a sudden wondered if it was the right time?

"DOLBY!" she called.

He had just reached the top of the second floor when he turned around on the landing. Grandma shuffled toward the foot of the steps. She looked up at her grandson, paused for effect, and playfully wagged her finger his way. "Now don't you go and storm off with your half-tail between your legs!" Dolby's mouth fell open and looked at his grandmother like a deer caught in the headlights.

10

FAMILY

"I praise you, for I am fearfully and wonderfully made.
Wonderful are your works; my soul knows it very well."

—*Psalm 139:14*

Steele had a lot of time to think during his nightly dog walks. On this one, he thought about how loud his dad had just yelled at him for no good reason again. Many of the pit bulls that came to his dad had gone through abuse of some kind or another. He didn't realize it, but that's partly why Steele enjoyed the dogs so much. He could relate to being treated unfairly and felt something of a kinship with them. He also thought about Dolby . . . a lot. One thing he didn't think about was *why* Dolby was on his mind so much. If he was able to reflect on it, he would've realized that his rage toward Dolby was a coping mechanism in order not to feel the pain of his own mistreatment. His loss of control at home only made him want to control Dolby all the more.

Besides, in his mind, Dolby had completely humiliated him in front of the school and deserved what was coming to him. It was the first week of school when the whole conflict started. Steele had talked back to the teacher and was made to move his desk to the front of the class next to Miss Daken, just under the whiteboard. It was after lunch and for some reason, Steele had pocketed a mustard packet from the lunchroom. He doesn't know why, but in his anger at the teacher, he kneaded the mustard back and forth in his hand. He continued to massage the packet until it worked a hole into the top, causing bright yellow mustard to explode across her board like a painter spraying color from his brush across a canvas. Impulsively, he grabbed an eraser and in a moment of thoughtless panic, began to "erase" the mustard off of the board. But, of course, the action only caused the condiment to be smeared into more of a mess. Dolby held his laughter back when the mustard first squirted. But the erasing attempt was too much. Dolby erupted into laughter that only encouraged others in the classroom to do the same. The biggest and toughest kid in the school was almost reduced to tears. He vowed at that moment to make Dolby's life as miserable as he was made to feel. Yet, Dolby kept getting the best of him. He knew he was somehow to blame for calling on the blacktail to pin him against the wall of the principal's office, which, he remembered well, resulted in an even more humiliating wetting of his pants. He also knew a message had been sent to the herd of deer to chase him away at the farm that night. Steele had never run from anything or anyone. As he walked, he concocted a plan that would either humiliate Dough-boy in front of the school, or expose whatever weird thing was going on with him and the animals, or both.

Geema handed Dolby a glass of stale Coke that no longer fizzed. She sipped hot tea from a mug. They sat across from each other in the living room, both sinking low in ugly furniture from the 1970s. The old woman smiled, enjoying Dolby's confusion. He finally found the words. "What do you know about half-tails?"

"Enough to know that my grandson is one."

"How do you know about half-tails?"

"Oh, Sweetie. Your old Grammy wasn't born yesterday. This 'ole bag o'bones has been around the block a few times. I've known about half-tails since before you were a twinkle in your parents' eyes."

"How did you know I was a half-tail?"

His grandmother didn't answer with words. She just sarcastically smiled and pointed a bony finger toward the bay window that overlooked the backyard and woods. In the far cornfield, at least two dozen deer grazed lazily. Just outside the wooden fence, Snowflake and a few other fawns played something that looked like tag. To the right of the barn, another dozen or so whitetail was nearly invisible against a brown background of tall grass. If you looked closely enough, there were lone bucks of varying species staggered every few hundred yards around the property's distant perimeter. If one didn't know any better, they carried themselves like Secret Service agents surrounding the president. Punctuating her point, Geema laughed, "There are less animals at the Wanesville Zoo."

Dolby felt more important with every answer to his questions. "How long have you known?"

"Honey, I've known since you were knee-high to a grasshopper. You've had a knack with deer ever since I can remember. Only those who are familiar with half-tails would have picked up on it."

"Are there others like me? Others who can communicate with animals?" Dolby asked.

"One never knows, dear. Could be. That circus lion tamer could be one. The zookeeper and veterinarian and wildlife photographer—all could be half-tail. So, be careful what crazy cat-lady or professional dog walker you make fun of. They could be just like you—blessed with an ability to talk with their kind for some greater purpose.

"So, you've known one before?"

She slurped her tea with self-importance. "Your great-great grandfather, my Grandpa Clarence, was the first in the family that I know of. He was a half-tail to the fox. As a little girl, I can still remember all the different types of foxes that hung around—Red fox, Gray fox, Fennec foxes. My favorite was a little arctic fox that we kept as a pet. My grandpa took it in as an injured kit to nurse it back to health. Once she got better, she just never left the house. I'll never forget listening to my grandaddy and Cotton yipping and barking back and forth. And the stories! Now that you understand, have I got some stories for you! He always said that half-tail ability runs in the family. I doubted it until you came along. I wanted so badly to have the gift, but no matter how hard I tried, I could never make it happen. Just goes to show that it's a talent that's only given and not manufactured from within. Looking back, though, now I'm not sure I want it after all."

"Why not?"

"Well, because where a lot is given, a lot is often asked. You have been given this gift for a reason, and who knows what challenges you may have to face because of it?" Dolby didn't want to think about that, so he quickly asked another question.

"So, I guess I'm not that unique after all, huh?" His grandma joined him on the hideously orange couch.

"On the contrary, my boy! Think about it. You are probably the only living half-tail deer, making you . . . what? One in 8 billion?! But, even if you didn't have this power, you would still be the only one like you in the world, making you—that's right—one in 8 billion. Each person alive is like a snow-flake—no two are the same. When he heard the word *snowflake* it made him think of his new friend. Through the window, he could see Snowflake jumping the fence over and over for no apparent reason. "So, if you really think about it, we are all special, with a unique mix of abilities that nobody else has. I think the bible calls it being 'wonderfully made.' Listen," she got real serious real fast. "It's really important that no one else knows about this. Besides, very few will believe you anyway." Dolby nodded his head, remembering the ridicule he received when he tried to tell one of his class-mates. Even so, he desperately wanted others to see how important he was. The genius was his, after all, he thought. I can do with it what I want.

They sat in silence, both reflecting on the great responsibility that was on Dolby's shoulders. It was too much for him to think about and his mind wandered to other places. He leaned into a great bear hug and sighed. "I miss Mom."

Geema sighed in response. "Me too, Dolby. Me too."

Dolby was surprised at the secret thrill he felt having someone his own age—and his own species for that matter—to talk to. In fact, given his general awkwardness with people, he was way more comfortable with this arrangement than speaking to others face-to-face. He typed,

ok the password worked

He suddenly had the urge to tell his secret.

do u mind if i call u Dell?

11

SKUNK

"It's hard to enjoy practical jokes when your whole life feels like one."
—RICK RIORDAN IN THE LAST OLYMPIAN (2009)

It was unusually mild outside for the middle of a Michigan October, so the kids at Gomer middle school were allowed recess in the fenced-in playground after they finished their lunch. Most kids gobbled down their food as fast as possible, so they could maximize their play time. Dolby, too, wolfed his down, but only in order to have more reading time. He planted himself on an out-of-the-way bench all alone as usual—except that he wasn't alone, and he knew it. He was fully aware of all of the eyes upon him from the woods beyond the fence. With each day, there seemed to be more. Dolby worried that something big was coming sooner than later due to the influx of herds into Gomer. At the moment, though, he felt completely protected despite Steele and his friends sharing the same lunch hour. Shadow Muzzle was the most noticeable of the forest guardians that dotted the thick undergrowth. He also saw some male deer that he had either just met or recently heard about. There was a gigantic Rocky Mountain Elk with the biggest rack of antlers he had ever seen, who he knew to be Monster Horn. A Manitoban Elk from Canada called Canuck hid nearby. He was glad to see Gus, a Mule Deer and a Red Deer named Red Velvet. Mortimer Moose had just arrived, although not very quietly. He was most excited to see a Tule Elk from California named Wapiti, who, he was told, was legendary among the Whitetail. He felt like a movie star surrounded by bodyguards. The problem was that the increase in security meant that a potential threat was also increasing, making it a little hard to enjoy. No caribou were present. He knew they were assigned to protect Fantasma.

Dolby began to read and became absorbed in his book so quickly that he didn't notice two older boys sneaking around behind him. As silent as an assassin, Steele laid down on his stomach under the bench and grabbed two ends of a rope, tying each off in a loop. The other ends had been secured around the legs of the bench ahead of time. One of Steele's partners in crime waited for the okay and pretended to fall into Dolby's back so that his body lurched forward, and his legs swayed under the bench. The ropes were quickly lassoed around his feet. The thug apologized to Dolby as if it were an accident and then moved away to give Steele room to work. The bully had stolen a megaphone from the Phys Ed teacher's office and inched it close to Dolby's unsuspecting ear. With a quick click of the trigger and a whine of the bullhorn, Steele's voice trumpeted not only through the playground, but also directly into Dolby's eardrum. "HEY, PIG-BOY! DOUGHY ONE! WHATCHA READIN'?!" Dolby screamed and jerked forward. It happened so fast that he didn't have time to break his fall with his arms. His face pitched forward, landing firmly into the black playground mulch with a splat. The surrounding pine trees came alive with snorting and wheezing. But even with revenge on their minds, the bucks knew they couldn't attack. It would give both them, and Dolby, away. Dolby for his part also knew that he could not call for help for the same reasons. There were simply too many student witnesses. Steele had him where he wanted him. All of Steele's friends, and most of his enemies, couldn't help but laugh at how ridiculous Dolby looked with his face covered in black shavings. Steele laughed the hardest, of course, fully enjoying the humiliation that was now Dolby's instead of his own. Steele pointed the megaphone in Dolby's direction once again, "WHERE ARE YOUR FOREST RATS NOW, DOUGH-BOY?! HAHAHAHAHA!"

Dolby laid there, his face black with mulch and red with embarrassment. The usual feeling of helplessness and fear returned. His mind raced through his options, but none came to mind. He couldn't summon the help of the stags and there were no adults on the playground. All he could do was take it. Shadow and the other bucks could not.

Steele stood over him, celebrating his victory. He didn't hear the stomping of the blacktail coming from behind the fence. Shadow was sending a message, but not to any of his own kind. By this time, Dolby had gotten his feet freed from the ropes, which was timely due to what he caught in the corner of his eye. Like an overfed Ninja, he rolled away from Steele, and dove in the opposite direction. He may not be an athlete, but that didn't mean he couldn't be athletic when he had to be. Steele sensed that something was behind him, but it was too late. He turned just in time to be sprayed up and down by the business end of a skunk! He coughed and gagged and spit as the skunk waddled away back under the fence and into the bushes. The entire playground emptied of choking students like it was the last bell before summer vacation. Steele, too, took off on a sprint over the fence and toward home. He continued to gasp for breath through the pungent odor that he could not run away from. He peeled off his shirt as he ran, hoping that would help a little. Dolby covered his nose with his shirt as he, too, jumped the fence. The security detail remained in the woods and he wanted to thank them. They found a clearing where they could all talk and remove themselves from the stench of the schoolyard. A circle formed as Shadow Muzzle introduced him to each creature he hadn't yet met and re-introduced him to those that he had. It was disorienting for Dolby to move so quickly from the world of the no-tail where he had no importance, to the world of the whitetail, where he had more than he could believe. He moved from laughing stock to half-tail star in a matter of a few feet. "Now for hero of hour, Dolby please meet Stinkerbelle!" All of the deer stomped their feet with approval and snorted while Dolby clapped. The skunk shuffled to the center of the circle and bowed in each direction.

When he turned to face him, Dolby kneeled and using a baby voice—a natural reaction to the cuteness of the skunk—said, "Thank you so much, Stinkerbelle!" Dolby was shocked to hear a high-pitched squeal in response.

"You're welcome, Dolby!"

He looked at Shadow with both confusion and excitement. "Am I half-tail to the skunk, too?!" Shadow Muzzle tried to keep a straight face, but the uncontrolled giggling of the rest of the animals broke him. From behind Monster Horn leaped a spotted deer, who also burst into laughter. It was Snowflake who had just pretended to be the skunk. Dolby quickly under-stood that he was again the butt of the joke. The difference was, it felt good to be teased this time. The boy yelled, "Snowflake!" and proceeded to tackle the deer. They wrestled on the forest floor to the music of chuckling. Dirt and leaves were now added to the mulch that still covered his face.

When things settled down, Dolby had a serious question to run by the group. "Don't get me wrong, I am very grateful for all of your help. Shadow Muzzle defended me in the principal's office. Snowflake and the does came to my rescue at Farmer Brown's, and now you came to my aid against Steele once again. I'm a little confused, though. Wasn't I supposedly blown by the wind to be of help to you and not vice versa?" Canuck, the Canadian elk, was the first to speak up.

"Who's to say, eh? The ways of the Windmaster are often mystery. Maybe you were sent to help us, or maybe we were sent to help you."

"It doesn't matter either way," Red Velvet added. "What matters is that we are in this together." Dolby inhaled deeply at the thought of being a part of something bigger together with all of them, and then exhaled to know that it didn't depend only upon him.

"But remember, Dolby here for reason," Shadow offered, "all of us here for reason."

Mortimer the Moose spoke up with the deepest sound Dolby's ears had ever heard. "That's Truuuuuuuueeeee," he mooed, sounding like he was singing bass in a barber shop quartet.

After a few moments of silence, Gus, the mule deer changed the subject. "I reckon y'all agreein' wit' me that the winds of change they be a'comin'? Do any y'all gather that this youngun Steele got sumtin' to do wit' any of it?"

They all thought the same thing, but Wapiti made it verbal. "Could be, Gus. Could very well be."

Steele cursed under his breath all the way home, and even impressed himself with one creative insult in particular when he coughed out calling the skunk a "STUPID FART KITTEN!" Steele was so consumed with anger that he did not catch the irony that a skunk had just met another skunk face-to-face. It was a Friday, so Steele had plenty of time to wash the stink off of his skin and clothes. Unfortunately, the stink underneath the skin and clothes remained. He also had plenty of time to plan his next move.

do u mind if i call u Dell?

sure i guess! wat should i call u?

how about h.t.

ok . . . what does that stand 4

um . . . i'll tell u later

Day after day, the messages continued. At the same time Dolby was growing more trusting of Dell, Dell began to ask more questions of Dolby. The temptation to have someone know how important he was had become more than he could bear.

im ready 2 tell u what h.t. stands 4

ok . . . i won't tell anyone

promise?

of course

u r not gonna believe me tho

try me!

its gonna sound weird

thats ok . . . im used 2 weird i am weird 2 remember? lol ur secret is safe with me

ok . . . h.t. stands 4 half-tail. lemme explain

12

ALARM

"... a moment settled and hovered and remained for much more than a moment. And sound stopped and movement stopped for much, much more than a moment."

—*JOHN STEINBECK IN OF MICE AND MEN (1937)*

Geema often allowed Dolby to spend the night in the tree fort knowing full well that he was perfectly safe in the wild surrounded by his animal bodyguards. He had since outfitted the blind with a blow-up mattress, blankets, and a pillow for his personal slumber parties. But on this night, he was not able to slumber. Snowflake, and many of her friends, were sound asleep below the big Oak tree, and he had no one to talk to. It was two weeks before Halloween, so his mind wandered to trick-or-treating. Would he go this year? He hadn't gone in a couple of years because despite the candy payoff, it wasn't worth going out alone. He tried to brainstorm ways in which he could disguise a few of his deer buddies so they could go door-to-door with him. Of course, he could think of no safe way and quickly dismissed the idea. He grabbed a couple of comic books, but had read them many times before and tossed them aside. Even the soothing serenade of frogs and crickets wasn't making him drowsy. The alarm clock screamed one o'clock in the morning. He pulled the tree stump stool up to the window facing one of the open fields and stared out for a while. Dolby knew there was activity under the moonlight but didn't see much of it. He did hear an owl hoot. Coyotes yipped in the distance. Raccoons were chattering. He gave up and opened his fireworks chest, taking mental inventory.

He hadn't fired any off since just after the discovery of his gift. A couple of weeks ago, he was sitting in the tree fort and mindlessly shot off an explosive through one of the window openings. Dolby did not know at the time that Snowflake was hiding behind a tree just next to the Oak. The young fawn sprinted away from the explosion in a panic. When Dolby called out for her, she returned cautiously. "Why do you have a thunder stick?" Dolby understood that she was talking about a gun.

"It wasn't a thunder stick—it was a firework."

"Why are you trying to work fire?"

"I wasn't. Fireworks are kinda like fun, loud noisemakers. They really don't make fire or hurt anybody." Dolby argued at the time. "I'm sorry I scared you. I won't use them again." He blew out the candle that he used to light the wick to prove to Snowflake that he was serious.

He missed messing around with them, but he didn't want to startle any of his newfound friends. Fireworks had always relieved stress for him somehow, even though he wasn't exactly stressed out at the moment. In fact, he was unusually content. But he still wanted to light one off just for fun. He fought the urge, not wanting to alarm the forest dwellers. He ran his fingers along the red cardboard casing and wick of an M-80 explosive, imagining how much louder it would sound right now against the quiet night. Dolby knew they were so deafening that the military once used them to simulate exploding bombs during training. He also knew they were illegal to purchase. He racked his brain trying to remember how he had gotten it. It had been some time ago since he was saving it to use on a special occasion. Eight more were buried in the chest. He vaguely remembered a military veteran friend of grandpa's slyly sneaking them to him. He clutched it with his right hand and held it up in front of his face. With his left hand he pretended to light a match and ignite the wick. He could almost hear the sizzle of the rope burning down toward the firecracker. He imagined that he had seconds to throw it before it blew up in his hand. He quickly tossed it across the room where it banged against the wall and rolled down harmlessly to the floor. Then . . . BOOOOM!!! All at once, the woods around him exploded with sounds of panic and activity. Something big had awoken the forest, and it wasn't his firecracker hitting the wall. He grabbed the flashlight and ran to the window. Whatever it was that had caused the chaos, Dolby sure never heard anything. All of the initial bustling and rustling in the brush was silent once again. As far as his flashlight beam could shine, all Dolby could see were glowing eyes in the darkness looking for the source of what roused them. Dozens of deer heads popped up from their hidden beds frantically looking around as fast as their ears swiveled. It seemed that the entire woodlands had heard something loud and scary, and now the entire woodlands was attempting to find what it was and where it came from.

Dolby climbed down to investigate. By the time his feet hit the ground, he was staring at the butts of seven muscular stags who formed a circle around Dolby and the Oak tree. They faced outward with their massive racks almost touching as they stood guard in the case of an attack. Shadow Muzzle snorted orders to the others as they scanned the moonlit surroundings. Dolby felt at the same time great comfort that he was being protected so well, and great discomfort that he was a potential target that needed that kind of protection. They remained at attention and Dolby remained behind the barrier of horns for the better part of an hour. Finally, as the tension began to lessen, Dolby felt that the question on his mind could safely be asked. "What exactly did you hear because I never heard a thing?"

Shadow grunted a quick, "Cover me," to his comrades, and backed up into the circle as the deer reshuffled their positions. "Half-tail no hear because half-tail not full whitetail or blacktail. My kind hear sounds that are too high for Dolby. All deer heard it tonight."

Dolby knew that deer can hear high-pitched noises that humans are unable to detect, remembering his dad's deer whistles that were attached religiously to every vehicle they owned. "Then what exactly woke you all up?"

"That is question Shadow cannot answer."

Red Velvet joined them. "It was a loud siren-like noise that lasted about fifteen seconds. Its frequency was so high that it not only woke us up, it also was painful to the ear—like an alarm of warning or something."

"And yet there was no movement that accompanied the alarm, eh?" added Canuck. "And I know you all noticed that there were no clues to be found in the wind. Nothing to detect; no scents to decipher, were there?"

"Noooooooooooo," crooned Mortimer Moose. By now, they had all abandoned their posts and were discussing the oddity together.

"What do you think it could be?" asked Dolby.

Wapiti took over. "It is strange that there was no activity of which we are aware that followed the siren. You may be tempted then to think that it means nothing. But, I can assure you, even without evidence this is certainly *something*. There is a reason the Windmaster has gathered us all together here. There is a reason Half-tail is with us. A signal has been sounded. We may not know what it is or what awaits but be sure that this is only the beginning."

Dolby shared with Dell a little more each day. To his surprise, no matter how crazy his stories sounded as he typed them, the response was always supportive. In fact, he or she that was on the other end believed Dolby about everything. No matter what was shared, Dell was amazed and only wanted to know more. Of course, this made Dolby want to finally meet his pen pal.

```
                              should we meet sometime?


Hmmmm . . . i'm not sure wood it ruin what we have
now?

                                                  maybe


i kinda don't want 2 lose this friendship. i mean if
we met this could end. plus i have a lot more ques-
tions

            it is fun having this b r little secret


yes one more thing h.t. if we do end up meeting can
we keep this going? also lets never even talk about
these messages so it never ends & stays r secret



                                          sounds good
```

Dolby felt so accepted by Dell that he withheld nothing from him or her. Even with their agreed upon arrangement, he still longed to meet his friend face-to-face.

13

FRIEND

"A friend may be waiting behind a stranger's face."
—*MAYA ANGELOU IN LETTER TO MY DAUGHTER (2008)*

The next week and a half were a whirlwind for Dolby and the forests of Gomer. The next night after the siren incident, Snowflake woke Dolby up in the middle of the night. Dolby's room was on the second floor of Geema's farmhouse and it faced the backyard, barn, and woods. Snowflake stood under his window and, under the cover of the hedges, bleated as if in danger like the first time they met. Dolby slid open the window to find his fawn friend whispering to him to come down. They walked in silence to the back of the barn. The cool night air stirred Dolby from his fog. He looked at his watch. "SNOWFLAKE! It's three o'clock in the morning!" Every time he heard himself the name "Snowflake" out loud it reminded him of the conversation with his grandmother. No two snowflakes are alike. Everyone is made special and unique. He has been made special and unique? He was beginning to hope that were true. Snowflake wasted no time in explaining the situation.

"Three hours ago, we heard it again—a loud and painful blare. Twenty seconds this time. It's the second time in just three days. Just like the first one, there didn't seem to be anything connected with it. There was no further noise, no smells, and no other clues—just some weird signal. Shadow sent out scouts to case the woods for anything unusual. They came back with nothing to report, even though a second siren sounded about thirty minutes later. Shadow sent Gus, Red Velvet, and Canuck to base camp to seek Fantasma's advice. Do you think it could be a warning to try to spook us?" Dolby had no idea. If he had to guess, the only guidance to come from Fantasma would be to wait and see what happens next.

It wasn't the last time they heard it. Every night, two signals returned as loud as ever accompanied by the same questions. After the fifth time, a group of them gathered at the river by the tree stand where they drank in both the water and the beauty of the landscape. Gus, the Mule Deer, piped up, "Well, how do? Shore is a right nice day. Say, you don't reckon we are jus' bein' paranoid 'bout this ruckus we keep a'hearin'? We t'aint seen a lick 'o nuttin' since we got here. Ain't been no varmint no how. Mebbie 'tis some kinda no-tail machine? What'choo think half-tail?"

Dolby had been so wrapped up in seeing it as a threat to the white-tail that he hadn't considered that it might be something coincidental. The wheels were turning. "I guess it could be some sort of aircraft that produces the high-pitched sound as it flies by."

"But, we've not seen or heard anything in the sky when it happens," Red offered. "Could there be any other explanation, Dolby?"

"It could be some kind of backup generator that hums when turning on or something. Or maybe a factory noise from a neighboring plant?"

"Dern tooting, it could be." Gus had no idea what Dolby was talking about but was just looking for an excuse to leave. "If nuttin' comes up soon, I'm fixin' to skeedaddle and git outta Dodge."

Shadow Muzzle had heard enough. "No one go anywhere until Fantasma say so. The wind no lie. Something coming. We wait until right time." The rest agreed, but Gus wasn't convinced. As the days wore on, the alarm sound started to become unalarming. Like clockwork, an alert would be sounded two times each night consistently between the hours of midnight and three in the morning. The second alarm would follow the first approximately twenty to thirty minutes later each time. They had gotten so used to it each night that they were being both awakened from their sleep and lulled to sleep all at the same time.

All morning long, Dolby couldn't wait to tell Dell about the newest alarm, and the latest conversation with the deer. He had overslept and didn't have time before school. He waited until his classmates were cheek-deep with PB & J and potato chips. There was nobody around when he snuck into the library. He looked behind him as he turned the corner to head down the hallway that ended at the out-of-the-way computer. A small, skinny girl tried to make herself skinnier to avoid running in to Dolby, but he bumped into her nonetheless. Most people would have called out, "Watch it!" or "Excuse me!" But she was so quiet that it hadn't occurred to her to use her voice. Dolby jumped back in surprise. "Uh . . . sorry." He began to connect the dots. "Wait . . . you aren't . . ." The girl smiled. "Are you . . . Dell?" She smiled again and looked down at her work boots. He could already tell that she was as shy as he was awkward. "I am H.T.!" he excitedly announced. He suddenly realized that based on the way they had left things, he may have already crossed the line and said too much. He had seen her before in school, but she was the type that was so timid and bashful that she all but made herself invisible. She continued looking down and twirling her long, dark hair when all of the computer conversations came rushing back to his mind. He hadn't noticed it before, but it had always been about him and his special abilities and his exciting adventures. They had not once talked about her. They had the whole rest of the lunch hour left, so Dolby asked, "Do you want to sit down and talk?" He asked her about what grade she was in—sixth grade just like him. He asked her about where she lived—on the same road but two miles away. He asked her what she liked to do—riding horses and reading. He continued to ask questions and getting lots of one-word answers for the remainder of lunch. "Boy, she sure is shy," Dolby thought. He could see why she liked their computer relationship so well. She actually spoke up with a question of her own.

"H.T.?" They both jumped as the bell rang.

"You don't have to call me that anymore. My name is Dolby. What should I call you?"

"What you called me before."

"Dell?"

"Yes."

"But, what's your actual name?"

"That is my actual name."

"Huh?" Dolby was quite confused.

"A-Dell," she mumbled. "My name is Adele—Adele Brown. My father is Farmer Brown." She did kind of look plain, like a farmer's daughter.

"Ohhhh. Wow. That's ironic!" She smiled. "Wait, did you have a question?"

She never got to ask it. Mrs. Krantz wobbled into the library, balancing on her cane. She yelled at them with her quivering voice to get to their next class. She seemed even crazier and more unstable than ever. Dolby thought that she needs to retire if the two quietest kids in school are bothering her this much. "Can we talk more after school?" Dolby couldn't believe those words just came out of his mouth. Maybe this friendship thing isn't as hard as he'd been making it out to be.

"I can't, sorry. I have to help my dad with the afternoon milking. Do you want to come over after dinner and help me hose down the milking parlor?"

"Sure! Is six o'clock okay?"

She answered with an embarrassed smile.

14

PROOF?

"Christian . . . entered the Valley of Humiliation overconfident
and puffed up with false pride . . ."

—*JOHN BUNYAN IN THE PILGRIM'S PROGRESS (1678)*

Even though Dolby could hardly contain his excitement at dinner, his grandmother would not notice—he was still as quiet as ever. He kept checking the clock. Of course, it wasn't the cleaning up after cows that he looked forward to—it wasn't even hanging out with an actual friend, though that was a part of it. What he was anticipating the most was proving to Adele—well, to *anyone*—that he really was somebody of great importance. He could almost picture her face as she watched how the deer looked at him and talked to him and even *listened* to him. He pictured her face admiring his. He then wondered if there was a way to demonstrate his abilities in front of the whole school?

He pedaled up to the same red barn where he had the run-in with Steele. Even though he was a few minutes early, Adele was already hosing down the floor of the milking area. It was a rectangular addition to the barn that had twelve milking stalls on each side for a total of 24 pens—what her dad called a double-12 parallel parlor. It was on the smaller side for a building where milking was done. But, then again, the Brown's farm was below average in size for a typical family-owned dairy farm. They had just one hundred head of cattle—mostly Holsteins—but that was plenty for the amount of work it demanded. Adele had already hooked up another hose and, without talking, he followed her lead in spraying down the filth. She waited until he was facing the other direction before she allowed herself to smile. The next time Dolby smiled was when they finished showering the parlor and hung the hoses on the wall. She was about to say, "Thank you," but before she opened her mouth, he blurted out, "Come on, I want to show you what I can do!" She hesitated until he asked with another smile, "Don't you trust me?" She dutifully followed as he jogged out the back of the complex, through the pasture and carefully under the barbed-wire fence that kept the horses corralled. He helped her through and led her over the creek which ran behind both of their houses, to a heavily-wooded hillside just to their right. He remembered there being a good-sized herd of doe hiding here before. As they neared, he was not disappointed. Though camouflaged nicely, he counted at least nine deer grazing under cover. They now lifted their heads and stared in their direction. Dolby recognized most of them and started happily calling out. "Hello, Princess! Looks like you've already got a good start on that winter coat, huh? Lookin' good! There's Willow! Hi, Willow. Hey, Speckles—I'd like you to meet someone. Come here for a sec, would ya? Where's Raindrop? Doesn't she usually run with you guys?" The more he talked, the more they stared, statue-like. He tried again, but this time there was more concern in his voice. "Actually, uh, can any of you just come over? I want to introduce Adele." The deer looked at him with such indifference that it made him feel stupid. Sweat formed on his forehead, and he got that sick feeling in the pit of his stomach. "Come on, guys. Don't do this. I just want her to see." Dolby's voice cracked. He marched closer, "Please? He then heard a familiar snort but strangely couldn't make out the word or phrase. At that, the deer all literally high-tailed it deeper into the forest and disappeared. One lone buck picked his head up, took one look at the two of them and stomped away, his black tail the last thing to be seen. That look—Dolby instantly recognized it as one of disappointment. Fantasma's words of warning flooded back to his mind, "You are NOT to tell anyone about your secret skill. It could put our kind in too much danger." It was supposed to remain known only to him, the deer, and the Windmaster. He stood there, tears welling up in his eyes, and feeling like he was going to throw up from the shame. Dolby was mortified. He could not face Adele and wondered if she would ever talk to what she would think was his lying face again. Without looking at her, he sprinted past toward the barn and sobbed like a baby as he raced away on his bike. He was halfway home when it happened—Geema's pot roast, potatoes, and carrots coated his two-wheeler.

It was starting to get dark, but Dolby longed for complete darkness—burying himself under his covers would do for now. Geema's farmhouse was just ahead, blurry due to the tears. He would not get there, though—not for a while. He sped around the last corner of the dusty, gravel road but standing right in his way, blocking the road, were two gigantic moose cows. He instinctively jerked the handle bars away from them, sending him hurtling down a single path into the woods and further away from his bed. He was going too fast to try to turn around and started to coast in order to figure out where to go next. At that moment, two young whitetail bucks emerged from the thicket, forcing Dolby down another wooded pathway. He didn't know why, but he started to panic as if he were being haunted by deer-shaped ghosts. He pedaled harder, only to be steered in a new direction by a Rocky Mountain Elk similar to Monster Horn. With each change in direction, he breathed harder and cycled faster. Was that a Red Deer? Did he know where he was being guided, or to whom? Was he just trying to run away from himself? He didn't know . . . maybe both? Watch it! A Mule Deer appeared out of nowhere. It was growing darker, especially in the thickness of the woods, but some silhouettes were easy to recognize. A male moose directed him left, followed by three large female Elk who sent him veering right and down a slight slope. As Dolby reached the bottom, the front tire skidded on a sheet of fallen leaves, launching his bike on a slide as if coming around third base and headed for home. Dolby was tossed off of the bicycle and was himself sent sliding right into the shins of a light-gray creature. Before the dust even settled, Dolby felt himself rising up into the air. A Caribou bull had lowered his head and scooped Dolby up with his rack, like a front loader moving dirt into a dump truck. Dolby was cradled by the u-shaped opening formed by both sides of the antlers, and he bounced and pitched back and forth as he was carried deeper into the brush. Two other caribou flanked him on both sides as they ascended a familiar pathway. The three breathed heavily, but nobody spoke. At the top, a system of stomps on the ground was followed by the opening of pine branches. Dolby recognized this as the base camp where he first met Fantasma, the albino whitetail. What he didn't recognize was the surrounding hillside. It was completely different, outfitted now with an elaborate system of fallen trees and dirt mounds that would make climbing any part of the hill a much more difficult endeavor. The base camp was turning into a military fort right before his eyes.

15

FORGIVENESS

Aslan: (about Edmund the traitor) ". . . and there is no need
to talk to him about what is past."

—C.S. LEWIS IN THE LION, THE WITCH AND THE WARDROBE (1950)

Dolby's vehicle climbed directly to the overlook. He was gently un-loaded and dumped onto the boulder where he had first spoken to Fantasma. The three caribou took their places to stand guard for the arrival of the white doe. Dolby braced himself for the worst. He had selfishly put the entire deer community at risk in order to look good in front of Adele. He had deliberately disobeyed the orders to keep quiet his secret. How could he think only of himself when entire species of animals were under threat? He was in deep trouble and knew it. If the elaborate tactics of getting him here were any indication, this was going to be a long night and a long conversation—a long one-sided conversation too, he thought. And if the business-like behavior of the caribou was also any indication, Dolby had better get ready to come up with some fast answers and explanations. Dolby sat on the rock with his head buried in his hands, awaiting the interview with great apprehension. The noise from the birch trees got his attention and he looked up long enough to see Fantasma Bianca striding toward him. She looked a little different to him—bigger, and more majestic—but softer. If he would've been told ahead of time that she would look different, he would've guessed that she would seem bigger, scarier, and darker. But, was his mind playing tricks on him? Because she clearly looked *whiter* than before—purer, maybe? In fact, so beautiful and vibrant was her complete whiteness that Dolby could not stand to look upon her any more. He lowered his eyes and head back into his hands and mentally tried to prepare for the conversation to come.

He heard soft footsteps, but no words were yet spoken. A warm burst of wind blew from the valley below and whipped hard against Dolby's frontside as leaves on the ground were disrupted into a flurry of twisting air current. The invisible wind moved in a circular, tornado-like path until it landed directly above Dolby. He was too afraid to look but could feel leaves flowing around his whole body and glancing off of him like a cyclone of confetti. It was a whirlwind of sensation that was oddly peaceful. The next thing he felt was something wet. It took the dying down of the leafy funnel cloud before Dolby could determine what was happening. Something wet had definitely brushed his neck. He opened his eyes to realize that Fantasma herself had lifted both front legs onto the boulder and leaned forward and nuzzled his neck and face with her wet nose. He allowed himself to be embraced. The tension in his muscles relaxed. His breathing slowed down and became deeper. He felt some more wetness, but this time falling down his cheek. He allowed himself the freedom to enjoy the moment. But not for long. A growing anger began to swell inside of him that was a surprise even to him. "NO!" he yelled. Fantasma stepped back. "I DON'T DESERVE THIS. I WAS WRONG. I SHOULD BE YELLED AT. I SHOULD BE PUNISHED." Fantasma simply smiled. She raised her front hoof and placed in on Dolby's shaking hand and tapped it gently up and down as if to say that it was all over—that he can now let it go. He buried his head in his hands once more, but this time it was to catch the tears. The only word he heard come out of Fantasma's mouth before she gracefully exited was to call Dolby's friend.

"Snowflake?"

The energetic fawn bounded in and couldn't contain herself. She hopped from side to side and back and forth as she awaited Dolby to let her escort him home. Snowflake was bouncier and bubblier than he had ever seen her. She talked the whole way home, which was welcomed by Dolby. He was mentally and emotionally exhausted and didn't feel like talking. He was still processing the words-free conversation he just had with Fantasma. He had to admit that Snowflake's jubilation was like an outward manifestation of what he was feeling inside. They had reached the back patio of his house and were about to say goodbye. It was dark by now, and Dolby, despite his weariness, had one more question for Snowflake. "So, how do I resist the temptation to tell others when I crave their approval so much?"

Snowflake shrugged her shoulders and matter-of-factly replied, "Once you truly know the Windmaster's approval than the need for the approval of others blows away in the wind." Snowflake let out a long bleat that Dolby thought served as a joyful exclamation point. But it was a signal of her own. From the neighboring fields, scores of deer, young and old flocked to Dolby's backyard and to him. Some came for a bow, some for a neck hug. Others gave Dolby a quick lick of the hand, and some just let him pat their heads. Still others were just content to be in his presence. As they stampeded away with great contentment, he wasn't prepared for one more visitor. A short figure stepped out of the shadows and smiled. It was Adele. Dolby didn't know what to say. Adele broke the silence.

"I was worried about you, so I came over."

Dolby answered, "Thanks . . . I, uh . . . I . . . I really can't talk about what happened earlier. I am not able to show you what I wanted to before."

"You don't have to."

"Wait . . . did you just see . . ."

"Yep! I watched the whole time. So, you really can communicate with deer, huh?!" She smiled. She had witnessed the exchange of wheezes and grunts.

"Yes, but nobody can know."

"It'll be our little secret."

Dolby continued to answer questions. He chuckled to think about how rare the questions came when they were together face-to-face. It so fits her shy personality, he thought. The questions came faster and more detailed—questions like:

```
how many deer do u think have come here 2 gomer
```

```
where do u c them the most
```

```
r they together or r they all over
```

He answered every question the best he could. He typed about the tree fort, the different species that were present, and the base camp. He knew he wasn't supposed to tell anyone, but she already knew so what did it hurt? Besides, he knew that she might be needed at some point, so she really should know everything.

16

PUMPKINS

"The barn was very large. It was very old. It smelled of hay and it smelled of manure. It smelled of the perspiration of tired horses and the wonderful sweet breath of patient cows. It often had a sort of peaceful smell—as though nothing bad could happen ever again in the world."

—*E.B. WHITE IN CHARLOTTE'S WEB (1952)*

Back and forth, back and forth, back and forth—all evening long went the tennis ball and the golden Labrador Retriever. Dolby and Adele sat on the second floor opening of the barn where hay was tossed down to feed the horses. Their feet dangled and swung in the crisp night air like they were awaiting a roller coaster ride to start. They took turns whipping the ball as far out into the horse pen as they could while also staying seated. Adele's farm dog Zeke loved running down the steps, through the aisle between the horse stalls, and out the back to retrieve the faded yellow ball. Reversing his steps, Zeke brought it back to them as if it were a race. Between throws, they could usually get in a question or two. In fact, "back and forth, back and forth" also described Dolby's many questions he had for Adele.

He didn't know if she was so easy to talk to because she was comfortable with silence, or because she used so few words in her answers, or because he felt like he already knew her—maybe it was all three. It was getting late, and the next day was a very hectic one on the Brown farm. It was the last Saturday before Halloween, which was always the busiest day for pumpkin sales in Gomer. Adele's job, with the help of Dolby this year, was to empty the two-acre pumpkin patch of all the best pumpkins and replace the ones that get bought. It was an all-day job to accommodate the pumpkin demand before Halloween, which was just four days away. Dolby knew he should leave, but he took advantage of the fact that his grandmother now assumed that if he wasn't home, he was at the tree stand.

"Does your Mom work?" he asked as he pried the tennis ball free from the jaws of Zeke.

"No."

"So, she's a stay-at-home mom that helps out on the farm?" Strings of dog drool flew out the hayloft opening along with the ball.

"Yep."

"Do they like being farmers?"

"Yeah . . . they love it. I think my dad likes being his own boss."

"Do you know what he likes to do the best?" Dolby had barely wiped the saliva off before it was time for another toss.

"I think he likes breeding the cattle the best. He's gotten to be kind of an expert in animal husbandry."

Dolby laughed. "HA! Your dad's a husband to animals?!" He knew it sounded immature the second it came out of his mouth, but he quickly recovered. "That's cool, though."

"Yeah. He teaches a college course once a year at Michigan State's College of Agriculture. I think it's called 'Improving Cow Genes' or something." Zeke's ball rolled away. Finally giving up, he collapsed in a panting heap tight against Adele's leg. They both followed his lead and laid back as well and were now staring up at the stars through the hay door. They were both pretty tired. "Genetic Improvement of Domestic Cattle?—that's it!"

"So, what does all that mean?"

"I guess just that he knows how to get the best animals to mate so the calves produce better milk and meat when they are old enough."

"And maybe so the cows get bigger and stronger and survive better?"

"I think?" They laid on the dusty, hardwood listening to the squeaking of bats and the swoosh of their wings flying overhead. It must've been close to midnight when the two new friends accidentally fell asleep.

The next thing Dolby remembers is being awakened by Zeke growling out the door of the hayloft into the night air. The dog never barked but kept growling quietly almost as if in fear. Dolby looked at his watch—it was three in the morning. He said something to the dog and fell right back asleep. The kids both snapped awake at the sound of the rooster crowing. It was six in the morning and they had to get the tractor ready. The pumpkins needed to be set up in the side yard by the time people started arriving. They ran down the old stairs, peeled the cobwebs back from their faces as they shook them also from their drowsy heads. Adele showed Dolby how to attach the trailer to the 1975 green and yellow John Deere tractor when Farmer Brown's pickup truck slid to a dusty halt right outside the barn door. He was too angry to acknowledge Dolby's presence. "They did it again—stupid deer." The kids looked at each other. "I just came back from the lettuce field and the fence I just installed did nothing. They jumped it and still got at the lettuce and cabbage. I hate those ratty animals—always ruining the crops. Even if I were to hunt them down, there would still be too many to keep away." He kept muttering to himself as he loaded pumpkin signs onto the truck bed. "At least they have been leaving the pumpkins alone."

Not knowing how to respond, both kids remained silent as the tractor pulled away—Adele driving and Dolby hanging onto the railing in the trailer. They traveled slowly down the gravel road over the bridge, around a bend and toward the secluded two acres of pumpkins. This would be the first of many trips as Adele figured that they would be loading up to 300 of the best vegetables. They had already harvested one hundred of the pumpkins, which had been picked through at the roadside stand over the past week. Her dad's voice materialized amid the static of the two-way radio he insisted that she carry while working the farmstead. "Adele—make sure you are watching for black rot. The customers are expecting the best pumpkins."

Adele spoke back into the Motorola, "Okay Dad." She clicked off the radio, "You big grump." Dolby decided to have some fun with his friend. He yelled from the back. "You know he heard you, right?—you didn't take your finger off of the button!"

"Seriously? NOOOO! Ugh . . . he's going to be even grumpier now."

"I'm just kidding!" A baseball hat went flying past him.

They bounced and rumbled past the wooded opening to the pumpkin patch when Adele brought the machine to an abrupt stop. Dolby went tumbling forward in the trailer, having let go of the railing to retrieve the cap. When he looked up, Adele was sprinting toward the opening of the patch. She had stopped running by the time Dolby got there. He joined her in staring out at the open field. A click of the walkie-talkie interrupted the silence.

"Uh . . . Dad . . . we've got a major problem at the pumpkin patch. Get over here—NOW!"

17

INVESTIGATION

"It is a very serious thing, Edith," said Mr. Zuckerman . . .
"We have received a sign—a mysterious sign . . . has happened on this farm."

—*E.B. White in Charlotte's Web (1952)*

"WHAT IN THE . . . how is this possible?" Clayton Brown yelled as he scanned the mainly orange horizon. "Two acres of pumpkins just destroyed?" The farmer shook his head. Pumpkin fragments littered the patch as if Halloween just threw up. "Two acres of pumpkins smashed to pieces? Who would do this?" He walked the perimeter asking no one in particular, "How?" He took off his Tractor Supply baseball cap, scratched his head and asked, "Why? . . . We just lost thousands of dollars." He bent down to touch the vines and ground. Turning to his daughter, he begged, "Did you hear anything last night? Did you see anything?" Adele shook her head no. "This is bad," he mumbled. "This is real bad. What are we gonna do? We depend on our pumpkin sales, and now . . . nothing. I've got to call Chief Kowalski." Dolby and Adele looked at each other with big eyes, both knowing what the other was thinking. Geema, and the rest of the town, suspected that the police chief was wrapped up in something illegal with Steele's dad since he could often be found at the old hotel where Swampy Canis lived. The kids did not want him involved in the investigation.

"Dad, wait. Can we do our own investigation before getting the police involved? I mean, I don't know, all the rumors about the chief, ya know?"

"Sorry, honey, this is thousands of dollars' worth of damage we are talking about here. You gotta understand, I *have* to get the authorities involved." Farmer Brown had heard the rumors too, but hardly thought Kowalski might be behind some damage to a small plot of farmland. But, his daughter rarely spoke up and when she did, he listened, knowing it must be important. "I guess I could call in a favor to Kyle." Kyle Robinson was a high school friend of Clay's, a Gomer police officer, and someone he trusted. "But I can't guarantee that he won't submit an official report." Clayton Brown would ask if he could keep it quiet for now. "I'm going to go call him." Farmer Brown still hadn't got into the habit of carrying his cell phone while he worked. The pickup peeled away leaving Dolby and Adele alone in the field. Dolby rushed to grab his backpack from the trailer and pulled out his binoculars. He carefully studied the area. There was an obvious circle of destruction around the entire two-acre pumpkin patch—the vines were completely trampled flat in a circular pattern. Another oddity was that not one pumpkin was left intact—there had to have been close to a thousand pumpkins all reduced to smithereens. The binoculars stopped moving and zeroed in on the very middle of the crime scene. Dolby twisted both wrists as he focused the field glasses.

"Whoa."

"What is it?" asked Adele.

"Not sure . . . hand me my backpack. Stay here."

Dolby carefully tiptoed upon pumpkin vines not wanting to leave footprints. He made it to the middle only to discover a pile of a few off-white bones. He combed through the skeleton parts with a stick. They were larger-sized animal bones with not even a smudge of blood anywhere, as if they had been licked clean. One of the bones was clearly a skull, and the another was probably a femur—the biggest bone in the body of most mammals. He knew he didn't have much time before Mr. Brown returned. A decision had to be made—and quickly. Did he trust the police with this evidence? He didn't know Officer Robinson, but he sure knew Steele and his dad and did not want these clues to get into the hands of anyone who sided with them. Opening his pack, he tossed in three bones, zipped up the book bag and retraced his steps. He placed the bag back in the trailer just in time to see Mr. Brown return with Officer Robinson riding shotgun.

After the two men did some investigative work of their own, they were left with more questions than answers. The kids heard phrases like, "No tire tracks," and "No animal paw-prints," and "No pumpkins untouched."

Officer Robinson had never seen anything like it. "So far, we haven't received any unusual reports from any other farm. It seems this—whatever this is—only happened here." He, too, scratched his head with the eraser end of a pencil. Looking at his pad of paper, he scribbled something else down. "A circle of flattened pumpkin vines; a thousand or so pumpkins either missing or destroyed; no animal tracks; no evidence of a vehicle—if I believed in UFO's, I might be tempted to think this was one of them crop circles done by an alien aircraft from outer space." He chuckled at the ridiculous thought. Turning to his school buddy, he said, "Clay, I can sit on this for a little while. But if you find any more evidence, I may have to make it official."

"I understand—thanks."

Dolby was itching to continue the investigation with the help of Shadow Muzzle and Snowflake and the others. Clay Brown was so frazzled by the events and thinking about what to tell his customers that he barely noticed the two kids running away. They had to cut through a cornfield and turn left over the creek using a rickety bridge in order to get to the treehouse. They were met by Snowflake along the way who just wanted to play. The fawn was just as happy to take a message to base camp. Dolby asked to meet with Wapiti and Shadow Muzzle at the Oak tree. "Hey, Snowflake?" Dolby yelled. The spotted young deer stopped and looked. "Did you hear the alarm last night?" Snowflake nodded her head.

"Yes, but we have been hearing it every night. It's okay, though, because there are no scent clues yet." Dolby wondered whether Adele's dog Zeke had growled at the high-pitched noise the night before, or at something else that he sensed or heard in the dark.

Wapiti sniffed and moved the bones around with his nose. "Can't be sure, because these are a little unusual. But, if I had to guess, I think these are dog bones of some kind."

Shadow Muzzle added, "many dogs possible. Which dog?"

"Not sure. I don't recognize them."

Dolby and Adele looked at each other. "Could they be bones of a pit bull?"

"Hmmmm. Could be, Half-tail. But it would have to be an extremely large pit bull. Again, there is not enough evidence to determine what type of dog we are talking about here. Tell us more about where you found them."

Dolby acted as translator as the two middle schoolers explained in great detail what they saw at the pumpkin patch. Dolby stopped mid-sentence, realizing that the stags never questioned the presence of a no-tail. In the middle of all of the craziness, Dolby had forgotten that Adele was an out-sider and wasn't supposed to be in on it. "Wait? Are you okay with Adele knowing all of this and being a part of it?"

Wapiti laughed, "We have known about Adele for a while, maybe even longer than you have, Half-tail. We were concerned at first. But, Fantasma says that anyone our Half-tail trusts, the whitetail will trust as well. She is as welcome as is the great Dolby." Dolby translated for Adele but left out the word "great." Adele smiled. Dolby also smiled inside, surprising even himself that he didn't need be praised at that moment.

That evening, the two kids sat on white rocking chairs on Geema's front porch trying to make sense of things. Her house was off the beaten path enough that not too much car or foot traffic came by. But tonight, a dark figure approached in the distance. Steele Canis was walking three pit bulls down the country road and toward the house. They were safe on the porch, but not too far away to notice a few things. First, the three pit bulls were again different dogs than Dolby had seen before. Secondly, each of them had some sort of injury or cut or visible scar. The third thing that both of them witnessed was a smile across Steele's face as he sarcastically waved to them on his way by.

18

FIRESIDE

"I sit beside the fire and think of people long ago,
and people who will see a world that I shall never know.
But all the while I sit and think of times there were before,
I listen for returning feet and voices at the door."

—*J.R.R. TOLKIEN IN THE LORD OF THE RINGS: THE FELLOW-
SHIP OF THE RING (1954)*

The nights were getting colder and this one was no exception. Dolby and Adele were driven back inside where they were welcomed by hot chocolate, warm chocolate chip cookies, and a roaring fire. It wasn't quite yet cold enough for a fire but tell that to Dolby's grandmother. She sat quietly reading in front of the blaze, secretly content with the sound of munching from the kitchen. The kids continued their feast and joined her in the living room. Adele was greeted with, "Hello, sweetie! It's so good to see you Adele! How *is* your mom and dad?" She put her book down.

"Mmmmm," Adele's mouth was full, "Pree goooo."

"Good. That mother of yours is such a dear. And your father—as hard a worker as they come. A shame about them pumpkins. What is this world coming to?" The rumor around town was that vandals had smashed their way through the pumpkin patch. "Have some more cookies, dear. You could use some meat on your bones." She didn't have to twist their arms.

They returned with a plateful and had to catch a few upon plopping back down on the couch.

"Geema?"

"Yes, grandson?"

"Can you tell us more stories about Gomer and stuff?"

"Of course, honey. What would you like to hear?" She loved that he cared about the town's history.

"Um . . . I don't know. Like, tell us about Mr. Vanderflunder." Dolby was fishing for information about Officer Robinson but couldn't lead with that. She might get suspicious. He was a terrible actor but hoped Geema was too old to notice.

"Sure. He and I go way back. I believe the Vanderflunder's came over from Cedarton. His family all worked the mill, but not a young Barney. He was gonna make it in pictures. Started out in Vaudeville even though Vaudeville was on a slow death. But he was determined to make it. Moved to New York City after school but was a major flop—couldn't make it there. Came back to Gomer in the sixties and got his teaching degree. Even though he worked his way up the school system, he was always kind of an embarrassment to Margaret and Otis for some reason." She suddenly realized she was telling stories about their principal. "Now, don't you be sharin' what your old Geema is saying."

"Yes, ma'am. What about Mrs. Krantz?" Another smokescreen before asking about the cop.

"Oh, good old Edith. You know we was best of friends growing up— like peas and carrots. She married Cliff right outta high school and we kinda went our separate ways as folks'll do. Cliff was some kind of chemist for a while—worked in a lab—but could never hold a job for long. A genius, that one—smart as a whip. Always inventing things and getting patents. I shouldn't be telling you this, but something happened and they was never the same." Dolby didn't care. He just wanted to get to Officer Robinson. "When her only son was sixteen years old, he died in a tragic car accident. From that moment on, she became crazier than a loon—at least that's this old biddie's take. The only thing keeping her somewhat sane was working at that middle school. They couldn't take living in that house on Main Street 'cause of the memories and bought the old abandoned Grist Mill north of town—you know the one? The place that everyone says is haunted? They became loners after that. Sad story."

Dolby wasn't social enough to know how to make a polite transition, but he tried. "Bummer. What about Officer Robinson. Do you have any stories about him?"

"Sure." Gomer was small enough that she had stories about everyone. "Kyle Robinson grew up here." She didn't seem to be catching on. "Come from a stand-up family. His mother was president of the school Parent-Teacher Organization for, oh, must've been thirty years. We still play Bridge together. And his father—what a hoot! He owned the general store in town and Kyle worked there since he was a whippersnapper. He went off to the service after school and was gonna make a career out of it. But, he missed his hometown—which is fancy talk for sayin' he met a girl—and came back to work the police force. He's good people, that one." Both Dolby and Adele were satisfied. Adele was not as suspicious as Dolby—she trusted her dad's judgment. Dolby, of course, had trouble with trust. Adele normally didn't initiate conversations, but she felt comfortable enough to ask the question. After asking it, though, she remembered why she didn't speak up more often.

"Mrs. Withers?" Geema's maiden name matched her current physical condition.

"Yes, dear?"

"What is your daughter like? Dolby won't talk about his mom."

Dolby glared at his friend. How could she? He shoved the plate off of his lap and stomped upstairs to his room in a display of anger that Adele had not seen. He clearly refused to talk about his mom. The upstairs bedroom door slammed shut.

Adele realized she had just crossed a line. "I'm sorry. I shouldn't have asked that." Geema sighed.

"No, dear. It's okay. It's been a rough year for the Hart family, that's all. Dolby is not yet ready to talk about his mother. But, if you are going to be a friend to him, you must know." Adele wasn't sure about that but braced herself for the worst. The damage was done, she figured, so she might as well hear the story.

"Dolby's mom had to raise Dolby on her own ever since he was about eight years old. His father left her for another woman and completely abandoned them. Karen did her best, juggling her work and raising him as a single mother. But, she had her struggles. Serious health issues came which caused her to lose her job. She was already disillusioned with life when the windstorm hit. A huge cherry tree in their front yard was struck by lightning and landed on their house. Dolby and his mom were holed up in the basement when it happened, so they were safe. But, Dolby still has nightmares to this day about that awful storm. Well, she didn't have insurance, couldn't afford to fix the house, and so were forced to move to Gomer to live with me. I am not exactly sure what happened to her after that, but she kinda went off the rails. Started acting funny like she was itchin' to leave. Some folks suspected drugs or alcohol. She told Dolby in a tear-filled goodbye that it was for the best that she go, that she loved him but had to do this, and that I will be takin' good care of him. She would say things like, 'I can't help you here anymore,' and 'I'm doing this for you,'—that kind of stuff. She also said that she hoped he would understand someday, and if not, maybe she could explain when he was older. He won't talk about it, but he did confide in me a couple of months ago that before she left, he asked her where she was going. Her tear-filled answer was, 'Wherever the wind takes me.' For some reason, that really stuck in Dolby's mind. Ever since, Dolby has been crippled with fear during storms and threatening weather. Of course, he is still trying to make heads or tails of being abandoned by both his dad and his mom. I'm guessing he feels abandoned by God as a result because he won't go to church with me anymore. So, we plug along. We are both hoping to see her again one day when she is in a better place."

Dolby had avoided the computer for many days after Adele asked his grandma about his mom. He had calmed down, but still wanted to avoid the topic. So, when he checked the first message, he was relieved that it didn't come up.

```
so, who do u think is behind the punkins
```

```
                    idk prolly steele u saw how he smiled @ us
```

```
yeah
```

19

TURKEYS

"A cook she certainly was, in the very bone and centre of her soul. Not a . . . turkey . . . in the barnyard but looked grave when they saw her approaching."

—*HARRIET BEECHER STOWE IN UNCLE TOM'S CABIN (1852)*

Two weeks had passed since the pumpkin incident and all was quiet in
the world of the no-tail. Officer Robinson continued to investigate, but
no new clues had surfaced. He would have been very interested in three
hard, white clues that were tucked away nicely in a backpack in the bottom of a chest full of fireworks in a treehouse, hidden by Dolby like a dog
burying his bones. But things weren't so quiet among the whitetail. There
continued to be two loud signals that only they could hear each night. They
also continued to be false alarms as no scent or activity were detected. After
the scare at Farmer Brown's, they treated every alarm as if it were real.
Each night, a scouting detail of multiple deer were assigned to depart in
different directions to look for anything unusual—like night watchmen at
a museum. They refused to be lulled to sleep for the next attack. The trees
were increasingly bare, the air was getting colder, and Thanksgiving was
just around the corner.

School had just let out and Adele aimed her ten-speed for home when
the familiar black Ford F-150 pickup truck pulled up next to her. Farmer
Brown simply said, "Get in." His tone was serious. As she lifted her bike up
over the tailgate of the truck's bed, Dolby pedaled up.

"What's going on?"

"Nothing good," she guessed. After making sure it was okay with her dad, Dolby also hoisted his bike into the truck. He was embarrassed that it took longer and required more effort for him than it did for the skinny little farm girl.

"What did your dad say?" Dolby panted.

"Nothing yet." They turned east on Creekview Road and bounced along in silence away from school and town. The road followed the bends and turns of Cedar Creek that flowed on their left. The creek kept going, but the road veered right with Adele's farm approaching on the left. But the truck just kept going. Dolby's house was two miles ahead, and the white farmhouse also came and went. They traveled another couple of miles before her dad turned into a parking lot they knew to be Calhoun's Turkeytown. Normally at this time, the lot to Gomer's only tourist attraction would have been completely full. People flocked from surrounding counties to eat different turkey dishes in the cafe, shop in the general store, and see all of the turkey and chicken on the farm. Adele remembers many Saturdays playing on the playground and eating ice cream on a hay ride. But today, there were no customers. The only cars in the parking lot belonged to Jed Calhoun and Officer Robinson. Dolby breathed a sigh of relief that Officer Robinson had obviously intercepted the call before crooked Kowalski. Of course, Jed had heard about the vandalism at the Brown's, but he had called Clay because they shared a love of farming and frankly, he needed him. They had been sharing farming notes for over twenty years—like what kind of hay baler to buy, or what kind of herbicide worked best on corn. So, it made sense that the first call he made after calling the Gomer Police Department was good ole' Clay Brown. Farmer Calhoun escorted the men and two kids through the turkey barn where, if noise was any indication, the dozens of turkeys were safe and well. It was the back forty that was troubling. Jed Calhoun's turkey farm was free range, which meant that the chickens and turkey all enjoyed constant access to the outdoors where they had unlimited freedom to exercise and feed and play. The coop was always open, and it was up to the poultry as to when they wanted to be cooped up.

"The way I figure it, this fenced-in area is a good four acres. When I went to bed last night, there were around a hundred chickens and sixty turkey roamin' happy as can be. This morning when I came out to top off their feed, there was none. *None!* Not one bird—*anywhere.* I checked the perimeter and there were no holes in the fencing. I mean, who would do this? And so close to Thanksgiving? Whoever is behind this was either try-ing to hurt my profits or really could not care less. Tammy Lynn thinks it was those boys from Flemings Mill—they're bad news, that bunch. But, then there's this weird circle around the whole field. What d'ya make a'that, Kyle?"

The officer took one look. "That there is the exact same trampled-down circle as we saw at Clay's."

"This happened to you, too?"

"Yes sir. 'Bout a month ago. 'Cept I lost me 'bout a ton of pumpkin, and that ain't no lie."

Jed shook his head. "Why are these freaks targeting small farms anyway?"

Kyle Robinson decided to case the area. Like the Brown's pumpkin patch, there was still the unusual flattened sphere that appeared to be dropped out of the sky. Like the scattered pumpkin fragments, there were also bird remnants—bones and feathers—sprinkled around. Not too long into the search, he found something that wasn't present in the Brown case—paw prints. He searched around for the best examples and took pic-tures with his cell phone. He wasn't a hunter and didn't have all the North American animal tracks memorized, so he tucked that information away for later.

He then asked the others to fan out across the range and walk the entirety of the pen just in case there was more evidence to be found. Spread out on his right was Adele and her dad, and on his left—Dolby and Jed. They slowly walked forward together not really knowing what they were looking for. After walking for about five minutes, the policeman noticed something rather unusual. In what seemed like about the middle of the flattened sphere, were a handful of clean, white bones scattered in a small area. He yelled for the others to come see. When Dolby and Adele saw the evidence, they looked at each other wide-eyed. Kyle ran to his police vehicle and came back with an evidence bag. He carefully transferred each bone into the bag with a piece of cloth and what looked like large tongs. "Maybe this is the breakthrough we need. I'll get forensics on this right away."

Farmer Brown thought for a moment. "Hey, listen Kyle, how about if I do the DNA testing through the university? I can pull a few strings and get it back days faster than your precinct's crime lab." He lied. He had no idea how long the DNA analysis would take. Clay just didn't want Chief Kowalski to get his grubby hands anywhere near the evidence.

"Hmmm. It is tempting—the lab is pretty backed up and it would save me a lot of paperwork."

"Great! I'll make sure it gets to East Lansing first thing in the morning."

"Sounds good. Thanks." Officer Robinson sealed the plastic bag and handed it to Farmer Brown. The policeman took one more quick look around. He sure was baffled. Even so, he was ready to call it a day when Jed Calhoun piped up.

"Wait! What is that?" He crouched down to get a closer look. "Looks like metal fragments of some kind." Sure enough, as the five took a closer look, they all began to see small particles shining in the sun. They repeated the earlier process with a new evidence bag, but this time Officer Robinson kept this gem for himself. They were all speechless as if the wheels that were turning in their minds simultaneously shut tight their jaws as well.

Dolby broke the silence by whispering to Adele, "Follow me." He led her back to the pickup, handed down both bikes from the truck bed, and raced back west on Creekview. They rode past Geema's house on the right. She was bundled up on the front porch, rocking and sipping something hot. She waved as they hurried by, used to their comings and goings by now. Dolby skidded into the first entrance of the Brown's half-circle drive-way and continued around the house to the back path that led to the first crime scene. He dismounted his bike so quickly that both feet landed on the gravel while the bike kept sliding along on its side. He marched straight back to the middle of the pumpkin patch, where bones had rested before. He began his search, and sure enough, tiny pieces of metal littered the area. Dolby wondered how he had missed it before and picked up the biggest of the metallic shards, pocketing them for later.

As they walked back to gather their bikes, Adele said, "I think I have an idea."

20

STAKEOUT

"These hotels are not consoling places. Far from it.
Any number of people had hung up their hats on those pegs.
Even the flies, if you thought of it, had settled on other people's noses."

—*Virginia Woolf in Mrs. Dalloway (1925)*

They waited until 11 p.m. to carry out Adele's plan. Dolby had recruited Red Velvet and Canuck to accompany them as protection. They set out single file from the barn with the whitetail in front and Canuck bringing up the rear. Adele wisely thought that it was time to get some eyes on the Canis father and son to see if they were up to anything unusual, especially since Wapiti confirmed that the bones could be from a pit bull. The report from the Michigan State forensics department wouldn't be seen for at least a week or two. They crossed over the creek and followed it along on the north side since the Dew Drop Inn was also nestled north of the water in a secluded wooded area. They continued walking to the soundtrack of flowing water and singing frogs until they reached the small hill that was just east of the motel. The hill was so thick with trees that even without leaves on them, they were safe from discovery. They stopped at the highest point and settled in for a night of surveillance. It was not a school night, so they hoped if anything illegal was to happen, it would happen on a weekend, and they would witness it. Dolby and Adele each leaned against a tree while the two bucks laid down next to them. They could hear the muffled barks of dogs, and the occasional howl of wolves in the distance, but there was nothing out of the ordinary happening. They watched for a couple of hours, listening to the night sounds that eventually soothed them to sleep—even the bucks that were supposed to be on guard gave in. All four jerked awake to the sound of rustling behind them. They turned around to noises that were getting louder. Something was approaching! Canuck and Red stepped in front of the kids and lowered their heads, preparing for a fight. Louder and louder came the footsteps. The sixth graders covered their heads while peeking out through their hands. Canuck blew out a warning snort that Dolby interpreted as, "BEWARE!" Adele heard a wheezy grunt in response in the thicket. Dolby instantly relaxed and in frustrated English cried, "GUS!!" Poking his head out of the brush was the Mule buck.

"HOW DO?! Fancy seein' y'all here this time 'a night. Whatch y'all doin'?" he asked far too loudly.

"SSSSHHHHHH!" came the four-way reply.

"Well I'll be a monkey's uncle if it ain't Half-tail and his gal pal."

"SSSSHHHH! We are casing out this place for clues," whispered Red.

"Mind if I join ya?"

After some further explanation, the five resumed the stakeout. Gus had gotten their hearts pumping so fast that they had little trouble staying awake now. Dolby looked at his watch—two o'clock in the morning. He asked if they had heard an alarm yet tonight. They shook their heads no right as headlights appeared. It was a long driveway, so it took a while to tell what kind of vehicle it was. As it got closer, a visible gasp was heard on the hill as they all made out the silhouette of the rectangular light-bar on top of the car. It was clearly siren lights, on a black and white car with the words "Gomer Police" across the side. The spies watched the car slowly come to a halt at the top of the driveway. Emerging from the patrol car was an exhausted-looking police chief Kowalski, who strolled up to the front door and disappeared inside. If he had remained outside he would've instantly heard a commotion of whispers and grunts and movement from the little hill. There was lots of spirited talking—most of it at the same time. If he were a half-tail, he would've heard phrases like, "I told you so!" "I knew it!" and "Are you kidding me?" There was even, "That man is lower than a snake's belly in a wagon rut." As they continued the dialogue, another set of headlights swung toward the motel from the road below. Dolby tried to get the attention of the animals, but they couldn't hear him. He had to physically grab two sets of antlers to get their attention—"SSSHHHHH! Look!" He pushed their racks in the direction of the driveway. A long, white, eighteen-passenger van pulled behind the police car. Both Swampy and Kowalski came out to meet the van, and greeted a driver and his helper, both of whom were dressed in all black with black ski hats. They walked behind the van, opened up the back hatch, and two-by-two began taking turns carrying heavy-duty metal cages around to the back of the complex. Once the first two cages disappeared around back, Red Velvet jumped up and without saying a word, bounded down the hill and circled behind the van. He crossed the half loop of the driveway and parked himself behind a tree in the front lawn where he could get a good look at the inside of the vehicle. The four men came back out together, paired up again and each team removed another cage. Once the coast was again clear, Red retraced his earlier steps. There wasn't time to report his findings as the men returned for one last trip. The others anxiously awaited as the driver and accomplice slammed shut the van's back door and abruptly peeled away down the other half arc of the driveway. Dolby tried to keep up with the translating for Adele—"Injured or sick animals—six of them; had pointed ears on the top of the head and looked short and wide and full of muscle; big mouth—sharp teeth—scary eyes; their nose was flatter than Adele's Zeke; all different colors. I couldn't get any more read on them due to a lack of scent in the air. Some kind of—Dolby, I think what you call—dog."

"Pit bulls," Dolby answered. "Those are pit bulls, one of the strongest dogs known to my race. If trained properly, or even neglected for that matter, they can do some real damage with their powerful jaws." He didn't say it out loud, but he knew they were up to no good.

They sat there for another half hour just in case, but it seemed that the excitement was over. They walked carefully down the hill heading back in the direction of Dolby's. At the foot of the hill, they heard one more car engine. They scrambled back up the mound in time to see an odd-looking gray car turn off its lights. This time, nobody got out. Officer Kowalski and Swampy appeared from around back carrying a similar looking cage. They decided that inside must've been a healthy dog because it snarled and growled all the way to the open back of the car. Once placed in the bed, the vehicle's driver pulled away without saying a word to the two men. Adele, who inherited her knowledge of cars from her dad, explained that it was a Chevrolet El Camino, probably from the late seventies. They were considered trucks but were really just low-riding cars with a bed like a pickup truck. They all made careful note of the looks of the car in case they encountered it in the future.

hey y do u think Steele is being so nice i don't
trust him

i know right maybe he is on 2 us

could b i wonder y we didnt c him @ the hotel

???

21

CLUES

"Extraordinary observations require extraordinary evidence."
—*Astronaut Buzz Aldrin*

Thanksgiving had come and gone, and still no word from Adele's dad about the DNA tests. He told her that the results came back so oddly the first time that he had them sent back for another, more careful, examination. That was ten days ago, so it had to be finished soon. It was now the first week of December and the snow was beginning to fly. In recent weeks, Dolby had plenty of conversations with his white-tailed and black-tailed friends. There was still concern, but because the deer population had not really been affected much by incidents on a couple of family farms, the mood had gotten less fearful. Another week passed with plenty of fake alarms, but even the whitetail allowed themselves to enjoy the snow.

Dolby and Adele took turns gently hooking ornaments onto her Christmas tree while Zeke sprawled out next to the fireplace. Mr. Brown sat at the kitchen table reading the paper while Mrs. Brown took a steaming casserole out of the oven. The blizzard outside created a whiteout as Christmas music played inside. It was a charming family scene that Dolby never had growing up.

Officer Robinson, for his part, was busy trying to make sense of the pictures he had taken at the turkey farm. After discovering the animal tracks, he re-opened the Brown case in order to see if there were tracks on that property that were missed. He still didn't find any. It was probable, he concluded, that the reason no prints were detected was because the ground was covered with pumpkin vines and leaves that could have acted as a green carpet to hide any marks in the soil. He had borrowed a tracker's field manual from a local park ranger and got to work. It was obvious that the impressions in the field left by the creatures were those belonging to something in the dog family. They all showed imprints of four toe pads on top, and one heel pad underneath, which all came together in basically an oval shape—characteristic of all dog species. What was strange about these footprints was that they didn't match anything in the manual—and the manual was specifically for tracking North American animals.

The Brown family Christmas moment was interrupted by a cell phone call. The family couldn't help but overhear the one-sided conversation and tried to connect the dots.

"Hello . . . this is him. Oh, hey."

"Okay . . . right."

"Are you serious?"

"Are you sure?"

"The second time too?"

"Is that even possible in nature?" Mr. Brown listened. "I didn't think so."

"Okay. Yeah, send those over and I'll prepare Officer Robinson."

Mr. Brown tossed the phone on the table, put his hand under his chin and stared a hole through the opposite wall. "Clay, honey?" His wife's voice broke the trance. "Is everything okay?"

"No. No, it's not. That was the lab and the DNA results are quite unusual."

"You mean from the remains found at Turkeytown?"

"Yes. So much so, that they repeated the analysis using both bone and bone marrow DNA—and each confirmed the animal that made the attack."

"And?"

"And it wasn't an animal."

When snapping the pictures, Officer Robinson had the presence of mind to lay a five-inch pen next to the prints so approximate size could be determined. The manual stated that of those animals in the dog family, fox prints are typically two and a half inches long, coyote leave three-inch marks, while the paw-print of a wolf are around five inches. He had also found out that domestic dogs the size of pit bulls are generally four inches in length. The problem was that these impressions were so large that the pen in the pictures was just over half the height of the footprint, making them about 8 or 9 inches in length.

"Not an animal? What could it be then?" Mrs. Brown was as confused as everyone.

"I mean, it wasn't any animal that we are familiar with."

"Like a new species?" Adele and Dolby had joined the conversation. Mr. Brown was so consumed with the news that he had forgotten they were within earshot. It was too late now—they might as well hear it all.

"Something like that, I guess. Dr. Horowitz said that there was DNA evidence of both wolf and coyote in the sample."

"Meaning that wolves and coyotes mated? Does that happen in the wild?" Dolby asked. He was an expert in deer, not wild dog.

"Believe it or not, it's not terribly uncommon. I read an article recently that in places where the wolf population is declining—like it has been in Michigan in recent years—wolves will mate with a coyote if there are no wolves to be found. Their union creates offspring that is something called a *Super Coyote* or *Coywolf*. Apparently, they are on the rise in the Midwest."

Adele chimed in, "What's so unusual about this animal, then?"

"Well, they discovered that this animal contains a mixture of the DNA of not just two—but three different creatures."

The policeman kept researching. The paws of black bears could be eight inches long, and so could some of the big cats, but no dog species approached this large of a paw. Was there a new larger species of dog in the forests of Gomer? He did the math in his head. If a creature's paw is that huge . . . he shuddered to consider it.

Adele couldn't wait any longer for the answer. "What three types of DNA were in the sample?"

"Coyote, wolf and domestic dog," was the reply.

Dolby asked, "Again, what's the problem? If dog species can interbreed, why is it so alarming that there's also dog DNA in the mix?"

"Only that unlike wolves and coyote," Clayton Brown answered, "dogs will not naturally mate with wild dog species."

Mrs. Brown followed the logic and said, "So, this particular animal only exists because somebody has scientifically manipulated things to create a kind of a super dog."

"And has been doing so for generations of the animal. Those bones belonged to an animal that is closer in size to a large wolf—only larger. I didn't mention that the specific breed of wolf DNA is the largest one we know—the gray wolf. The scary question is why anyone would want to combine the size and strength of a gray wolf with the speed of a coyote—one of the fastest land mammals—and the most powerful dog we know?" They together considered the question in silence.

But, Mrs. Brown had one more question. "What kind of dog breed's DNA did he determine was mixed with coywolf?"

Mr. Brown answered, but he wasn't alone. Two other voices joined him in responding, "PIT BULL!"

Officer Robinson and Zach Brown talked on the phone later that night, sharing their discoveries. What they couldn't figure out was why the bones belonged to an animal that was closer in size to a large wolf, but the prints in the soil matched a creature that was far bigger—like that of a black bear.

Dolby woke up that night to the loud yipping and fighting of coyotes in the nearby woods. It wasn't an unusual occurrence, happening at least once every month or two. But this time, there was something odd about what he heard. There were other animal screams added to the chaotic noises that he had not heard before. He thought he heard domestic dogs barking and yelping, and cats meowing and screeching. Could it be the Pitcoywolves on the move again? The group had settled on calling these beasts a combination of the three animals—*Pitcoywolves*. He rolled over, thinking that he must have been dreaming. He looked at his clock—two-thirty in the morning. He nodded off momentarily. Then his eyes snapped open at the sound of the opening of the sliding glass door downstairs. It was an old door and made loud rubbing sounds when opened. He knew it couldn't be Geema— she was never up at this time of night. He listened closely as four animal feet took turns clicking on the hardwood floor below. He laid there in a panic trying to come up with a plan. There were no weapons nearby—his BB gun was in the garage and his fireworks were in the hunting blind. An M-80 right now would scare anything away, he thought. The clicking got closer—the animal was climbing the steps! The noises outside grew louder and more frightening. He sat up, resigned to the fact that his screams would be added to the night sounds. An animal pushed open his door with its nose. Dolby saw the four-footed silhouette in the dark and shrieked like he was about to die.

22

PETS

"The following morning, at the Council of Elrond. Gandalf and Frodo along with a
congregation of Men, Elves and Dwarves sit in a semi-circle around a stone pedestal.
Elrond: "Strangers from distant lands, friends of old.
You have been summoned here to answer the threat of Mordor.
Middle-Earth stands upon the brink of destruction.
None can escape it. You will unite or you will fall."

—FROM THE SCRIPT OF THE LORD OF THE RINGS: THE FEL-
LOWSHIP OF THE RING (2001)

Dolby ducked under the covers, still screaming in fear. The animal
nudged him hard. "IT'S JUST ME!" He peeled back the covers to see
his friend Snowflake. She was no longer covered in spots and was much
bigger, not just due to her thick, newly-grown winter coat.

"AAAH! You scared me to death! Don't do that!" Dolby breathed a
sigh of relief. "What is going on outside, anyway?"

"There's no time to explain. You've got to come with me—NOW!"
Dolby threw on some warm clothes and followed Snowflake out through
the sliding glass door. Dolby made a mental note to himself—it was time
to start locking the doors to the farmhouse. The second his foot hit the
ground outside, massive antlers scooped him up and tossed him onto a
broad, muscular back. Dolby instinctively grabbed ahold of each side of
the buck's rack and like the oddest motorcycle rider ever, accelerated into

the thick brush. Branches hit his face as he gathered his wits about him. It took a while for his eyes to adjust due to the lunging and bouncing of the galloping elk. First, he realized that he was swerving around trees at about the speed of a motorcycle on the back of Monster Horn himself. Keeping stride to his right were two more elk, and to his left were two white-tailed bucks. A quick glance behind him revealed Shadow Muzzle and four other deer he did not recognize. They were all racing forward with urgency, not unlike rows of motor-cross drivers sprinting down the home stretch.

Dolby yelled back to Shadow. "Where are we going?"

The blacktail grunted over the stampede, "Base camp." Dolby knew by the tone of his response that there were to be no more questions. Unlike the last time Dolby had been escorted to the base, there was no disguising the path. These massive creatures were on a mission to get there as fast as possible. Dolby felt like a prince being whisked away to safety by soldiers under the cover of darkness. The sounds of fighting he had heard earlier were getting harder to hear over the stampede of deer hooves. When they were the loudest, Dolby swore he heard not only the struggling of dogs and cats, but also the soft screams of a rabbit. But the bigger reason they were fading was because they were heading north and east away from the chaos, and the wind was picking up and snowflakes were battering Dolby in the face.

As they approached the entrance to base camp, the first thing Dolby noticed was increased security around the perimeter. New and larger deer were scattered around the base and top of the hill. To his right, he saw a herd of a couple of dozen exotic deer lining up to enter camp. He could be wrong, but he thought they looked like Sambar deer. Actually, he had to be wrong—Sambar live only in India and parts of China. They could only be here in Michigan if they came from a zoo or nature preserve. All of the deer now looked bigger and more impressive in part due to the think growth of winter coats. After a successful series of stomps on the ground, Dolby was escorted on the back of Monster Horn up the hill to where he had spoken with Fantasma. They walked by the overlook and into a more secluded part of the hilltop. Heavily hidden with pine trees, Monster Horn squeezed through to unveil an open area where deer of all sorts were gathering. To the left was the largest Red Maple tree he had ever seen in Michigan—it had to be 150 feet high. But that wasn't the most unusual thing about it. Even though it was the middle of December, it had not lost any of its leaves. Its branches extended out over the entire clearing, forming a red, yellow and orange umbrella of protection. Underneath, in the middle of the open space, was a flat, circular rock that was elevated about five feet high. Surrounding the rock was another circular elevation of earth about two feet high that looked like it could be used as a step to the middle boulder. It was void of any grass and looked as if it was a path that was frequently walked upon. Around that second raised circle were fifteen majestic creatures—all varieties of deer—that were lying down in the grass. There was no snow on the ground here—the canopy of leaves acted as a roof over the area. Monster Horn lowered himself down for Dolby to jump off. It was clear that he was to take his place in the circle. He sat down with Canuck and Wapiti flanking him on both sides. One empty spot remained around the ring, which was promptly filled by the late-arriving Sambar doe, who introduced herself as Zayan.

Everyone was silent, and instinctively knew that it still wasn't time for questions. But Dolby couldn't help himself. He turned to Canuck and whispered, "What is this anyway?"

The Canadian elk replied, "This is the Ring of Nod, eh? We are aboot to join minds to . . . SHHHHHH!" The deer all stood in a quiet salute as two white caribou entered, leading the way for Fantasma. She climbed up to the top level of the concentric circles and made a loud snort that Dolby didn't recognize. The rest of the company snorted in reply and laid down again following the example of the albino deer. Fantasma Bianca addressed the twelve tailed animals and the one half-tail.

"As you know, the winds have blown us together for such a moment as this. There is darkness hovering in the air and it is nearing. Our number is increasing every day. We welcome Zayan from the east." The newcomer promptly lowered her head before the white deer. "This only confirms that the stakes are getting higher. It has not been made known what the nature of this threat is yet. But, it is time for us to nod in agreement over a plan." The group blew air through their noses in approval. Red Velvet raised himself up and stepped onto the raised pathway. Fantasma nodded as if to say, "Proceed." Red began walking around the elevated circle slowly and measured his words.

"As you all know, we are at a great disadvantage—one that has never been encountered in the history of the whitetail. Our ability to perceive the surroundings using our sense of smell has been somehow disabled here. We arrive to this hilltop almost as sitting ducks without means of knowing when danger is at hand."

"What Red Velvet says is true," replied Fantasma as Red stepped down and returned to his place. "That is why I continue to send out scouts every night in all directions so that we have ears and eyes on the ground. But it is not enough. That is also why we have a half-tail among us—but we will hear from him later." Dolby grew suddenly nervous. "The wind also blows in reinforcements whose senses of smell have not yet been compromised. The Sambar have arrived this morning with reports for why we are gathered. Zayan?"

Even though the doe was from an exotic place, it looked similar to the rest of the whitetail, but with a smaller head, bigger ears, and light brown markings on its breast and back. Zayan began to walk around in front of them. "Greetings from far-away lands," she spoke with a much quicker pace and accent than they were used to. "Upon our arrival, we caught wind of an attack just west of here on a no-tail village." Dolby assumed that she meant a neighborhood. "The snow in this village was completely flattened by something in the shape of a sphere, and there were large prints like bear in the snow. The number of no-tail huts affected were fifty. But, no damage to any of the huts was discovered." She continued to walk, as if trying to make sense of things as she spoke. "A search party was sent out and reports that there have been casualties." The eyes of each deer locked on to Zayan. "Many animals belonging to the no-tail have disappeared. So far, seven dogs are missing." Dolby thought of Zeke. "Five cats are gone, and two . . . um . . . what you call rabbits have also vanished. The odd thing is, of the animals belonging to the no-tail that were outside of the trampled circle, none were harmed. Also, it is a good thing that there was a great wind tonight or else many more animals might have been out-of-doors." For once, Dolby thought of the Windmaster in a positive light—and was surprised at feeling thankful.

"Were there any bones found?" Fantasma was aware of the bones recovered at the turkey farm.

"As a matter of fact, yes. But none were from the human pets. Only a couple were spotted in the very center of the sphere. Also, bits of tiny, hard, shiny material were recovered." Zayan paused to see if there were any more questions and then stepped down.

Dolby was hoping that what came next would not. Fantasma looked in Dolby's direction and in front of everyone said, "Half-tail, without our sense of smell, you are the Windmaster's gift to us. Please tell us what you have been hearing from Him." Dolby froze as every eye stared him down. He had nothing to say—absolutely nothing to contribute. There was little moonlight, but he felt the heat of the spotlight nonetheless.

He stammered, "I . . . um . . . well . . ." Fantasma motioned with her head toward the elevated pathway. Dolby stepped up and started to walk. He had no idea what to say or how he could be of help.

23

COUNCIL

"I buried Little Ann by the side of Old Dan. I knew that was where she wanted to
be. I also buried a part of my life along with my dog."

—WILSON RAWLS IN WHERE THE RED FERN GROWS (1961)

It was six in the morning, but Officer Robinson had been up since two,
and looked like it. He was exhausted after receiving call after hysterical call about missing pets and fierce animal sounds over in the Deer Pass
subdivision. The whole department was involved now, and Kyle Robinson
was glad for the help. Thankfully, Officer Kowalski was off for the weekend.
He had been to the crime scene and seen the now familiar round, flattened
area and the bear-sized tracks in the snow. If the site had been a ten-acre
dartboard, he had gathered four bones from the bullseye. The two farmers
were there with him at the police headquarters at Robinson's invitation.
They were having a meeting of their own.

"I don't get it," volunteered Clayton, "I mean, what's this guy's end
game? He is developing an army of super dogs on steroids in order to destroy some pumpkins and turkey and a few pets? Doesn't make a lick of
sense to me."

"I don't know, but I'm thinking he's sending some sorta twisted message," added Jed Calhoun. "Think about it—you were targeted right before
Halloween when losing a pumpkin crop would hurt the most. I was next,
right before Thanksgiving, when my turkey business was at its highest. And

now, these poor families—losing their beloved pets right before Christmas. Gun to my head? I'm guessin' there's some kind of sick revenge thing going on as motivation. You know, like 'If I'm not happy, I'm not going to let anyone else be happy.' But again, what do I know? Just spitballin' here." Officer Robinson mulled that one over. The next big event on the calendar was New Year's Eve and then there weren't any more until Valentine's Day in February and St. Patrick's Day in March.

"There's another thing that is very curious," said the policeman. "The destruction started in a two-acre pumpkin patch. The next one was in a four-acre turkey pen. This one caused a good ten acres of damage for over fifty families. And why in the middle of a blizzard? If he was after killing the most pets possible, it wouldn't have been carried out in the middle of winter. I'm wondering if these are all some kind of practice runs for something much bigger and more devastating."

Clayton Brown chimed in, "So what do we have to go on?"

Jed Calhoun replied, "Well, we know that according to the DNA of the bones, there's some kind of breeding going on—with pit bulls as part of the equation."

"And we know Swampy Canis has some sort of operation up there with pit bulls and kennels," added Kyle.

"And Adele tells me that Swampy's son is always walking dogs that have all kind of cuts and scars."

Officer Robinson rubbed his hand through his hair. "I think it's time I get a search warrant to check out the Dew Drop Inn once and for all— seems to me that Swampy is our best lead. I'll talk to the judge first thing Monday morning."

Dolby walked the circle slowly, hoping that something would come to him soon. He decided to just start talking out loud in the hopes that it would turn on a light bulb in his mind. "Okay, so we know there have been three incidents. One at Farmer Brown's, one at Turkeytown, and now one at the Deer Pass development." That was all it took—he had an idea. Dolby stepped down and whispered something to Red Velvet, who nodded and followed him to the massive Red Maple tree. He whispered something more and Red began to carve lines in the bark of the tree with the points of his antlers—the trunk being wide enough to serve as a whiteboard. The buck stepped away revealing a line that went from the top left down to the bottom right in the shape of a curvy "L." "This is Cedar Creek. Up here in the north, it runs past the old mill, flows down, turns east and goes by the old Dew Drop Inn and downtown Gomer." The bottom part of the "L," just as it changed direction, made a hill-shaped curve under which the town was nestled. After some more whispers, Red stepped toward the tree and marked some more. Toward the bottom part of the "L," after it moved past Main Street and the school, were three circles to the south of the creek that Red Velvet had engraved, each one getting a little larger than the last. "The first circle is the site of the first attack—Farmer Brown's patch. As you go east along the stream,"—Dolby had picked up a branch and was teaching the class as if a tenured professor—"you come to the second site. This is Turkeytown. Continuing to the right even further is the third crime scene—the Deer Pass community. Each circle gets bigger representing the size of the area that was targeted." For a second, Dolby couldn't believe he was in front of an audience commanding their attention—something that he would have never done six months ago. Wapiti stepped onto the raised path, clearly catching on.

"So, what you're saying is, there is a pattern at work here. The attacks are not only getting bigger, but they are heading somewhere—east to be exact." Canuck also stepped up to the pathway and walked on the opposite side of the circle along with Wapiti. Dolby was surprised this was allowed.

"Are you saying, young half-tail, that all of these events are possibly preparation for bigger and more easterly invasions?"

"If you look at the map, it sure seems that way."

"Another thing," Wapiti added, "This village name—Deer Pass—do you think it was chosen for a reason?"

Fantasma nodded. "Wapiti makes a good point. Whoever is to blame is sending us a message of warning. They are trying to get our attention and to make us fear."

A lightbulb went off in Red Velvet's head. "As in, deer pass away?"

"Exactly." Fantasma continued, "Is there a specific pattern to the sizes of the circles that get flattened?"

"Using the measurement of the non-tail, the first one was two acres in diameter. The second was four, and the third was ten. So, each time the area that is the aim is approximately double the size of the area before," Dolby answered.

"What we need to look for, then, is an area east of the non-tail village that is over twenty of your so-called acres?" Zayan the Sambar joined the walking path.

"Yes."

A black-tailed buck that Dolby did not know stood at his place and couldn't help himself. He blurted out without entering the circle, "And right along water. Where could this be?" Dolby whispered to Red one more time. Red Velvet calmly drew a circle twice the size and just to the right of the Deer Pass spot. When the stag stepped away revealing the map, the rest of the audience gasped. Fantasma nodded slowly and answered gravely for Dolby.

"You, my friends, are sitting on the very location of the next attack."

The entire ring of Nod became silent as the weight of Fantasma's words sank down upon them. The talking pathway was now void of activity. All that could be heard was the sound of the wind blowing through the maple leaves, when suddenly, a silver caribou burst from the brush and sprung forward toward Fantasma. After bowing, the beast announced, "Excuse me, your wisdom. Permission to allow a visitor to approach the rock." Fantasma was caught off guard and hesitated. The caribou, knowing the importance of the guest, stopped being so formal. "Um, look, you're gonna wanna see this!" Fantasma nodded, granting permission. The caribou departed and came back immediately with a Sambar buck. The gigantic beast was cautiously carrying something laying across his antlers.

As he approached Fantasma's throne, he stated in a quick cadence and a deep voice, "I am Saluja from the east. The honor is mine," and carefully lowered his load onto the boulder. Another gasp came from the Circle of Nod. "This was found in the outer part of the circle at the no-tail village. We think it was involved in the attack but was trampled to death by others of its kind." For the first time, one of the beasts that was causing all of the chaos was before their very eyes. Its presence produced a thick fog of despair over the meeting. Directly in front of them was one of the monsters that they had just determined was after them. It was an understatement to say that it was ugly, and it had to weigh at least 300 pounds. It had the bushy tail and pointy ears of a coyote. It had the face and long snout of a wolf, and the coloring was a wolf-like gray and white. The body shape was that of a pit bull—musclebound, squat, and frog-like on a frame the size of a female bear.

In an unusual moment of weakness, Fantasma exclaimed, "What *is* that?!" Dolby knew, and stepped up to the walking path.

"I can tell you. Some of our best no-tail experts have determined that it is part wolf, part coyote, and part pit bull dog." He should've stopped there. "The combination of which is probably more violent than anything we've ever seen." What had started as a very hopeful meeting had disintegrated into a cloud of despair.

The urgency and intensity of things were really ramping up, and the next computer message directed to Dolby only confirmed that.

```
i was given something 2 give 2 u
i didn't want 2 lose it & i didn't want anyone 2 c it
so i put it in ur locker
```

```
                                            what is it
```

```
an emergency whistle that only deer can hear
u r supposed 2 use it if u r in danger & need help
```

```
                                ok i'll get it after this thanx
```

Dolby dialed up his locker combination and opened it to find a simple whistle hanging on one of the coat hooks. He looped it around his neck and tucked it under his shirt thinking that he better keep it on him at all times just in case.

24

POLICE

"Compassion for animals is intimately connected with goodness of character, and it may be confidently asserted that he who is cruel to animals cannot be a good man."

—*ALBERT SCHWEITZER*

That night, with a signed search warrant in hand, four men drove up the winding driveway in a car marked "Gomer Police Department" to the Dew Drop Inn. Officer Robinson wanted to keep the search party small so that word would not get back to Kowalski. Eight other sets of eyes watched Robinson, another cop, Adele's dad, and Jed Calhoun from the nearby hill. Adele, Dolby, Shadow Muzzle, and Snowflake wanted to see the fireworks, and Dolby secretly wanted to watch Steele wet his pants again. It was nine o'clock in the evening—they wanted to make sure Swampy Canis was going to be home. The four men knocked on the door and Swampy answered wearing a white lab coat. After a brief exchange, Swampy let the men in. The four friends waited for what felt like an hour before Dolby got antsy. "I'm tired of waiting—I'm gonna do some snooping myself. You two stay here and keep watch. Come on Adele!" She didn't think it was such a good idea, but as always, didn't speak up and went along. They peeked into the front window where five men were sitting in what was once the living room of the original house. Swampy talked while Kyle Robinson scribbled in his palm-sized note pad. They couldn't slip in through the front because they would be easily seen. Dolby motioned to Adele to follow him around back. From an aerial view, the old motel was shaped like an upside-down "V." The first floor of the two-story building served as the lobby where guests used to check in. This was in the top middle. Two wings were built off of the entrance, forming the sides of the pyramid. Each wing contained ten separate rooms that at one time were rented out. The kids ran around the wing closest to the hill and began making their way behind the building, peering through windows as they went. Each old motel room was now either a kennel where dogs barked in cages or had been remodeled for some kind of medical purpose. One room was clearly a place for performing operations; another looked like an examination room. Dolby shut off his flashlight before peeking into the next room because this one was fully lighted. A person in a white lab coat with their back to the window was in the middle of conducting some kind of experiment on a beat-up pit bull. As they got a closer look at the person, both figured it out at the same time—Steele Canis! Without thinking, Dolby grabbed the doorknob and burst into the room with Adele in tow. Dolby doesn't know why he did this, but later reflection told him he just wanted to catch Steele in the middle of some illegal act. It was hard to say who was more surprised—Steele or the two friends—because Steele stood there, knuckle-deep in the backside of a dog.

"What are you losers looking at?" came the shocked response.

"I'm really not sure!" Dolby said with a chuckle. He couldn't help it— his arch-enemy had his fingers up a dog's butt. "The question is, what are *you* doing?!" Dolby and Adele both gagged as the smell hit them like a slap in the face.

"For your information, this poor dog has impacted anal glands and I have to squeeze out the fluid or else it will get infected."

Dolby was still laughing. For the first time he wasn't afraid of the big eighth grader. "We all have our superpowers, don't we?!"

Steele was now red-faced with embarrassment. "Ha-ha, very funny. I *have* to do this—it's part of my job working for my dad. Can we keep this to ourselves? I've got a reputation to keep up at school."

Dolby thought for a moment. "How about if we promise not to tell anyone if you tell us what kind of operation you are running here?"

Steele thought for a moment. "OK—deal. But you can't tell anybody about that either."

"One favor, first?" Dolby asked. "Can we go to another room? This one smells like old fish." Steele finished up with the dog and put it back into its crate. He scrubbed his hands for what Dolby thought wasn't near long enough, and walked them to a conference room. They sat down and watched Steele's dad leading the policemen and farmers on a guided tour of the facility. Dolby noted that Swampy had a look like he had nothing to hide.

"So, what's so secretive that we have to keep on the down-low?" asked Adele. The question surprised Steele—he had never actually heard Adele speak before.

"We could get into big trouble if all of this got out so, again, can I trust you to keep it quiet?" Both kids nodded. "If not, I'll kill you both." Dolby now knew that he was all talk. "Okay, so when dad was going through Alcoholics Anonymous, he met a guy who was a part of a secret organization called *Dog Rescue Coalition*, or DRC. The DRC operates in rural areas where illegal dog fighting rings are active. They go undercover to find dog fighting, and then kidnap the dogs before they can be killed in a fight. That's where we come in. They bring the wounded dogs to us, and we rehabilitate them, so they can be adopted by loving families. We are kind of a makeshift Veterinarian hospital and adoption agency all in one. If anyone involved in the dog fighting business finds out about us, we could be in serious danger. These dogs are their meal ticket. Without them, no gambling money comes in. Not only that, this operation has been my dad's salvation—it gives him purpose which keeps him away from the bottle." He didn't say it but thought it—and away from abusing me. "The DRC trains us to nurse the dogs back to health."

"So, you're not breeding pit bulls at all?"

"Nope. We are only in the business of rescuing dogs and getting them healthy and to a good home. The DRC relies on donations and pays us for each dog we help."

"What about Chief Kowalski?" Adele asked. "Why is he always around and coming in at all hours of the night?"

Steele was surprised she knew. He looked back and forth at them through squinty eyes. "I can't tell you that."

Dolby smiled at his friend. "Adele, do they still have Show-and-tell in middle school?"

"Why?" inquired Steele suspiciously.

"Oh, it's just that while you were playing Chinese finger trap under a dog's full moon, I was snapping pictures." Dolby was lying.

"You wouldn't!" Steele glared at his nemesis to see if he looked serious. After considering his options, Steele dropped his head, sighed, and volunteered information that would save his image at school. "All right, but if this gets out, you didn't hear it from me. He's been down on his luck ever since his divorce. I don't know the whole story, but he made some bad investments or got into some gambling debts or something. Whatever it was, he asked dad if he could stay here until he gets back on his feet. He lives here rent-free in exchange for help with the dogs. He also works a lot of second and third shift security jobs in order to make some more money. I guess he's pretty embarrassed about it and wants to keep it quiet."

Everything seemed to be checking out in Dolby's mind. That would explain the white van dropping off injured dogs. It explains the gray El Camino picking up a pit bull. It also justifies why the police chief was always around and coming home at strange hours. Later, on their sleepy walk home, an owl seemed to be taunting them as it repeatedly called out, "Hoo. Hoo. Hoo." Both Dolby and Adele separately had the same question—Who? If Swampy and Steele are not to blame for the monster Pitcoywolves that are running loose in Gomer, then who is?

25

TREEHOUSE

"Our Father . . . who has given the gift of survival to the coyote, the common brown rat, the English sparrow, the house fly and the moth, must have a great and overwhelming love for no-goods and blot-on-the-towns and bums."

—*JOHN STEINBECK IN CANNERY ROW (1945)*

Both Christmas and New Year's had come and gone without incident, and school had started back up. Dolby pushed open the door to his house after school and was welcomed by his grandmother. She wasn't the only one there to greet him. Snowflake, too, was inside as a new fixture to the farmhouse. Ever since she figured out how to open the sliding glass door of the back porch, she now came and went as she wished as if she had her own personal doggie door. Geema loved the company while Dolby was at school, and Snowflake loved the attention. For Dolby, it was like having a sister. It did, however, prove to be a little hard to explain when Geema's friends dropped by unannounced! She bent over the dining room table poring over the pieces of a jigsaw puzzle spread out in front of her. Snowflake hopped over to Dolby, clearly too big to be inside, and wrestled him to the ground. Grandma fed the two friends celery and peanut butter and resumed her place at the table. Dolby watched her laser-focused concentration for thirty seconds as she worked to solve the 1000-piece puzzle. He thought that it was an appropriate picture of a lot of people in Gomer who were still laboring hard to solve the mystery. One piece of the puzzle was the person or people behind the attacks. And what was their motive? Another piece was the timing—when was the next big event to occur? Another was the location—was an attack really being planned at base camp where so many deer had now moved for safety? Another piece yet was why the attacks seemed to follow the flow of the creek. Dolby couldn't sit still—he had to follow his Geema's lead and search for puzzle pieces. He invited Snowflake to join him, but she remained behind, content to stay curled up on the couch.

There was still a little snow on the ground—but it had been a mild January, and unusually dry—and it had almost all melted away. Dolby didn't really know what he was looking for but decided to check out the creek for clues. He wasn't afraid to go out alone—none of the attacks happened during the day anyway—and he knew that wolves and coyotes were nocturnal beasts, only active at night. He also trusted his security team, who always seemed to be around even when he couldn't see them. Despite all of this, he still caught himself absent-mindedly rubbing the string of the emergency whistle around his neck as he walked along, making sure it was still there. He crossed over the bridge and began walking west along the banks of the creek. After about an hour, he retraced his steps, walked back an hour, passed the bridge and headed east along the water. He had made it about a hundred yards when he was stopped in his tracks by a deep growling sound. He looked up to see, blocking his path, a snarling black and gray wolf. Dolby's heart raced as he wondered what a wolf was doing in broad daylight. His question was immediately answered with one look at the animal. The wolf continued to growl, baring not only its fangs and gums, but also a white foam that sprayed with each bark and snap of its jaws. The wolf was rabid! Facts about the disease ricocheted around Dolby's head like a steel ball in a pinball machine. He remembered that rabies was a deadly virus in animals that is transmitted through the bite of another infected animal. He also knew that the virus gets passed through the saliva and eventually attacks the brain causing the creature to first become disoriented, then crazy and violent. Dolby quickly turned around and walked briskly back toward the bridge. The wolf followed behind, slowly gaining ground. Dolby sped up his pace, as did the frothing predator. He knew he had one option—to make a break for the closest place of safety, which was the treehouse. Dolby bent down, picked up a stone, fired it at the wolf and then took off for the Oak tree. After a quick stumble, the wolf tore after the boy, howling and barking, with its eyes looking as if they would pop out of its skull. Dolby made it to the tree and climbed the ladder in time to see the crazed creature leaping and biting at the air just below his feet. He made it to the landing, climbed the last remaining steps and latched shut the tree blind door. The wolf violently snarled and growled on the ground below, and Dolby breathed a sigh of relief. Then, the unthinkable happened—the wolf began scaling the tree. Up it came, gnashing its teeth in his direction once it made it to the wooden deck. Dolby acted quickly and shoved the tree stand table at the wolf. The stump landed a perfect blow with a loud thud against the animal's side, sending it tumbling over the edge and into a melty snow bank. The creature was slowed and disoriented, but quickly gathered himself for another attempt. Dolby knew he had only a couple of options left, and he went to work on both of them at the same time. He popped the emergency whistle into his mouth, blew into it over and over again in order to silently call for help as he tipped over the treasure chest. Fireworks tumbled out along with a candle and matches. Dolby lit the candle, grabbed an M-80 explosive and lit the wick. By this time, the beast was beginning his second ascent toward Dolby. The boy leaned over the opening and tossed the firecracker in the animal's direction. It went off mid-air and the loud noise knocked the rabid wolf off of the tree again. Dolby quickly threw another, and then a third all while blowing the silent whistle. It was working—the wolf was getting slower and slower to his feet but was still not giving up, further evidence of its insanity.

Because she was inside, Snowflake had not heard the high-pitched call from Dolby. But, all it took was one boom of the M-80 to jolt her off of the couch and outside. The young deer had remembered the explosion of the firework back when she heard the siren for the first time. Dolby had promised that he wouldn't set one off again, so she worried that something was wrong and that Dolby may be in danger. She sprinted and bleated all the way to the tree, calling for help from the surrounding woods. She arrived to the sound of two more firecrackers, and the sight of a demented beast trying to get at Dolby. The black and gray wolf slowly climbed up the ladder once more and was promptly knocked back down by what looked like a metal flashlight. By this time, the sound of rhythmic hooves came from all around. Buck after buck, elk after elk, and moose stampeded to the rescue. The first to arrive made quick work of the foaming animal, being careful to use only their antlers in order not to be bitten by the infected devil. The struggle did not last long, and finally the forest was free of the sounds of the crazed howling, growling, and barking.

Adele had been milking the cows, heard the commotion, and arrived in time to count fifteen of the biggest specimens of deer she had ever seen gathered at the foot of the tree blind. Dolby was talking at length, no doubt thanking them for their quick rescue. Dolby began to straighten up the floor of his fort when another noise caught his attention. He stopped and listened. His mind raced, his heart pounded, his breath quickened, and panic set in. Adele and Snowflake heard the noise too, but it didn't cause the same terror for them that it did for Dolby. He was obviously connecting some dots in his head. In the distance, from back at the house, came the familiar clang of Geema's bell announcing that dinner was ready.

"Oh, no!" he cried. "No, no, no, no, no, No, No, NO, NO!"—each "no" increasing in volume.

"What is it, half-tail?" asked Shadow.

"The alarms you hear—the signals you hear every night?"

"What about them?"

"THEY ARE DINNER BELLS. They call those demon dogs to feed."

"Sooooooo?" mooed Mortimer the Moose.

"Don't you understand? I JUST CALLED THEM TO FEED." Dolby kept shaking his head and repeating similar things under his breath. "I just called them to dinner. I just called them to feed ON US!" His so-called emergency whistle made the same high frequency sound as the alarms they heard each night.

Sure enough, the horrifying sounds of howling and growling and splashing were faintly heard from far away. Dozens and dozens of bear-sized Pitcoywolves rushed single-file through the shallow creek in their direction, and it was all getting louder by the second. Dolby couldn't stop. He grabbed the whistle, tore it off of his neck and threw it down. "This wasn't an emergency whistle—it was a set-up to DESTROY ALL OF US!" For some reason the stress of the situation compelled Dolby to find some-one to blame. He glared at his friend, who was staring up in stunned silence a few feet away from the tree. "ADELE? WHY DID YOU GIVE ME THIS WHISTLE?"

Adele shot him a look back of total confusion. "I . . . I didn't give it to you!" she yelled. "What are you talking about?"

"You told me on the computer where to find it!"

"WHAT COMPUTER?"

"THE LIBRARY COMPUTER!"

Adele shook her head and shrugged her shoulders, looking as confused as ever. Dolby collapsed and felt the acid rising up in his stomach. For the past five months he had been giving away all of the secret information—the location of base camp, the number of deer, and so much more—to somebody else! From the floor of the treehouse, Dolby screamed at the top of his voice to Adele and Snowflake, "RUN AWAY! . . . NOW!"

26

BATTLE

"For dogs encompass me; a company of evildoers encircles me;
they have pierced my hands and feet."

—*PSALM 22:16*

B y the time the reality of the situation sank in for Dolby and the fifteen male deer, it was too late for them to escape the snarling ring of monsters that were accelerating toward them in the distance. They were trapped. Fortunately for Adele and Snowflake, they were able to flee before being surrounded. Dolby was glad to see they were gone and out of danger. The deer had resumed their defensive position around the tree, ready to fight to the death. Dolby got his only weapons ready—a chest full of bottle rockets and firecrackers. He moved the already lit candle closer in order to ignite the wicks more quickly. As he picked up the whistle and looked it over, he had another awful thought—he was positioned in the middle of the circle and was now the target of all these hungry animals. It seemed that they had been trained to devour everything in their path until they reached the final bullseye—the animal in the center. Dolby then figured out what the metal pieces were that were scattered at each attack site. It must've been the siren and tracker the dogs were chasing down that eventually got destroyed in the final assault. Dolby realized at that moment that if he were correct, and if something wasn't done, his bones would be the only thing left in the middle of the trampled circle. He stuffed the whistle deep into his pocket.

They were sitting ducks, and he knew it. There was no way a boy with an arsenal of a few fireworks and fifteen deer, elk and moose could fight off the hundred or so bear-sized Pitcoywolves tearing their way toward them. How in the world could they survive? For the first time in his life, Dolby may have had an answer. The words of Fantasma rang in his ears—"The answer to all is 'the Windmaster.'" Dolby quickly raised his eyes to heaven and two words desperately fell out of his mouth—"Please help."

As the deranged beasts closed in, Dolby did his best to try and slow them down. He lit bottle rockets and shot them first out of a window toward one open field of galloping savages, and then out another toward the other clearing. He threw the remaining M-80's in both directions, but the monsters were so caught up in their violent frenzy that the fireworks were largely ignored. By now, a few of the wolves had arrived through the woods behind the tree fort, and in the strip of woods that divided the cornfields in front. The bucks clashed with the beasts and the forest was filled with howls and groans and yelps. They held their own inside the woods, but more were coming. Dolby fired a Roman Candle out one window, turned to light another one and slipped on an empty M-80 tube. His foot went out from under him and as he fell to the floor, the candle was knocked over onto a pile of old comic books. The small flame of the candle instantly grew as the pile of paper began to burn. Dolby tried to stomp out the blaze, but it only seemed to make it worse. The fire took hold on the wood floor and in a matter of just a couple of minutes, the entire wooden structure was an inferno of smoke and fire. Forgetting the danger below, Dolby's only option was to escape the danger in the tree by leaping down onto the flat landing. January isn't typically thought of as a common month for wildfires. But because trees shed much of their water during the winter, and because much of the surrounding woods were fir trees with flammable pine needles, the flames did spread like a wildfire. Soon, the strip of woods going north was ablaze in a wall of glowing red. Dolby sat perched on the branch and began to hear the cracking of the Oak tree. The entire tree was about to fall like a burning log in a campfire. Fifteen deer stopped their fighting and instinctively gathered at the foot of the tree to catch Dolby's fall. As the burning tower collapsed to the ground, Dolby leaped into the smoky black abyss not knowing where he might land. Monster Horn acted quickly and ran under the plunging boy. Dolby's chest smacked hard into the Elk's back knocking the wind out of him but breaking his fall. The Oak torch hit the forest floor to the right of where it used to stand, starting a line of fire on the ground.

Old, dried-out corn stalks erupted into flames in a northeasterly direction. If the circle of flattened earth was a pie chart, fire now blazed upward and to the right, forming a triangular piece of pie whose borders were aflame. The flames spread quickly blocking all of the deer, and about a fifth of the Pitcoywolves inside of a segment whose walls were ablaze. A clash ensued between the fifteen deer and about twenty devil dogs. The rest of the dogs were outside of the flaming vee-shaped area and could not get at Dolby or the various bucks. Monster Horn with Dolby on his back managed to keep away from the fighting. With the odds now much more favorable, some of the deer teamed up to kill one beast at a time while the others kept the remaining wolves at bay, until they were all left in motionless black piles on the ground.

Adele and Snowflake had now taken up a post at the Brown's barn just upstream from the tree blind. The red light of Adele's video camera blinked on with a beep. The crackling of the fire on both sides of them was too loud for Shadow Muzzle, Wapiti, Gus, and the others to hear what echoed through the forest next. Besides, they were too busy dodging left-over fireworks that were set off every few minutes by the out-of-control fire. Snowflake and Adele heard it from the barn, though. First came a distant howl that they both caught, followed by the same familiar high-pitched alert only perceived by the deer. Adele and Snowflake watched as dozens of bear-like brutes turned around obediently and headed south toward the creek in a single-file line.

Thankfully, the fire died down as quickly as it started due to the remaining patches of snow on the ground and didn't spread any further. As the smoke cleared, a boy laid face down on the back of an elk with tears flowing. He knew it was his fault that they had almost died that day. He had revealed secrets to the enemy. He had put the most powerful deer in Gomer in grave danger in what turned out to be an ambush. He had started the fire. As the deer traveled wearily toward base camp, Dolby examined the animals. Some were limping. Others were bleeding from bite marks. Still others showed signs of burns. Dolby couldn't stop the old feelings of failure from creeping in and taking over. He was supposed to be the great Half-tail, and all he did was screw everything up again. Wasn't he supposed to be helping the whitetail? He wanted to die. And some big help the Windmaster was, he thought. He felt foolish for asking for someone's help that either wasn't there or was only out to get him, like some kind of an invisible bully.

27

WIND

"Always there was this feeling of an unseen force, a fine net drawn round us with infinite skill and delicacy, holding us so lightly that it was at some supreme moment that one realized that one was indeed entangled in its meshes."

—SIR ARTHUR CONAN DOYLE IN
THE HOUND OF THE BASKERVILLES (1902)

Fifteen deer and one boy silently trudged through the snow looking forward to getting some rest. They would all find that rest, except for Dolby. The group was halfway to the base when they met another group of deer marching in the opposite direction. All seven of them had coats of white, while one had white covering every part of her. Dolby was surprised to see Fantasma and the caribou away from the security of base camp. But as Fantasma would later say, "It's always safest right after an attack." The albino deer demanded that the bucks continue on toward home, and all but demanded that Dolby join her entourage. He climbed on the back of the largest of the caribou, a male named Yukon. They were venturing back to the smoking crime scene. They poked around in silence for a while—Fantasma was interested to learn exactly what had transpired. She sat down on the ground at a spot that overlooked the ashes of what was once Dolby's favorite place in the world—the tree stand. It made him even sadder to face it but took his seat on the tree stump that survived the flames. Dolby soberly looked around at the results of a forest fire that was his doing. They both watched smoldering fires flickering around them. Somehow, Fantasma knew. "You are angry with the maker of the winds, young half-tail?"

He wanted to lie. He bit his lip in defiance instead. "I asked for his help. See? It didn't do any good."

"What makes you think you didn't get the help you asked for?" came the reply.

"Because everything is ruined. My tree fort is gone. My friends are injured. And there are monsters still roaming the forests of Gomer. I'm supposedly 'blown' here for some big purpose, and all I do is make things worse."

"I see," replied the one they call wisdom. "But there is plenty you do not see. You are but a boy, and only see the little that a boy can see. He is Master—He sees all. Could it be, young one, that what has happened here today is itself serving a greater purpose which would have been impossible otherwise?"

"You're right about one thing—I'm not seeing."

"Think about it—no lives were lost. Yes, you sounded an alarm that put the whitetail in danger. But now we know more about the enemy than ever before. We know they travel by water to avoid footprint detection. Yes, you communicated to an enemy at your school. But now you are aware that same foe lurks behind what you call a computer. You also now understand that what my kind hear each night is a feeding call. And an animal in the center serves as a sacrificial lamb in order to guide the monsters to a certain location. These may all be important pieces of intelligence—puzzle pieces—that could be of use in the future. The battle may seem lost, but a war is made up of many battles. Just remember that you, even as a half-tail, do not see as the Windmaster sees. And the more you are able to see as He, the more of use you will be to His plans."

Dolby knew he had no argument.

"But there is one more thing that you did not see." The Albino wheezed hard and loud, calling a female caribou forward.

"I am Nanuk, from the north. The honor is mine." She nuzzled her nose under Dolby's hand. "A few of my kind watched the battle from afar, up on that hillside." She motioned behind her. "We were there to see if our service was needed. Something happened during the struggle that you didn't see or feel due to the chaos—it was something that changed everything. Do you remember when the tree hut was on fire and you climbed down onto the flat seat on the branch?"

"Of course."

"What you didn't see, we witnessed very clearly from on high. When the great Oak began to crack under the heat of the fire, it first started to lean toward the north. If it had continued on this path, it would have fallen directly onto the strip of woods between the two fields that was already on fire. This would have exposed you and our friends to all of the wolf dogs. It would have been sixteen against ninety or one hundred, and you wouldn't have survived. Instead, as the tree began to lean forward, a great and mighty wind blew from the west and north and pushed the fireball in an easterly direction to your right. This ended up creating a small area that was walled with fire that ultimately protected you and also made victory possible. You were saved by a great wind!"

Dolby wanted desperately to believe Nanuk. "Understand this," Fantasma said. "You only see with your own eyes. You cannot see what others and the Windmaster sees. When bad things happen, you blame Him and yet you do not see the whole picture." Fantasma added one more thing for Dolby to think about. "You are correct about one thing, however, and you will soon see. The Master of the winds *is* actually out to get you—just not in the way you are thinking that he is." Fantasma punctuated her statement with a big grin.

Dolby thought about that one in silence for many minutes. The gears that worked in his brain grinded to a halt when Snowflake hopped up. Dolby was surprised that the young fawn was given such instant access to Fantasma.

"Excuse me, your wisdom?"

"Of course, Snowflake. You know you are always welcome."

"Are you, um, done with Dolby? I . . . well . . . uh, have something to show him."

"The half-tail is far from being done, I can assure you of that! But I think I know what you mean. Yes, you may go."

Dolby and Snowflake bowed before the doe and walked away toward the house. "What's going on?" Dolby asked.

"You'll see. It could be very important. By the way," Snowflake asked with a smile as they headed home.

"Yes?" The boy squinted suspiciously.

"I thought you said that fireworks don't work fire or hurt anybody?" The fawn then repeated what Dolby once said using a goofy, dumb-sounding voice, "Kinda like fun noisemakers!" The deer kicked snow in his face, laughed, and took off running with the boy close behind.

28

ALLIANCE

"You can't stay in your corner of the forest waiting for others to come to you.
You have to go to them sometimes."

—A.A. MILNE IN WINNIE-THE-POOH (1926)

The two friends chased each other all the way into town. They ran behind Main Street and down back alleys, so nobody would see a young deer and boy playing together. Snowflake ran all the way up to the road that, if taken north, would have made a dead end into Main Street and the only traffic light in Gomer. Instead, she led her friend south, away from the heart of the little town, and into an industrial area known locally as Factory Row. Not that there were many working factories left any more—the only remaining businesses were metal shops, fabricating plants, and construction yards. With each step, Dolby felt increasingly vulnerable. He knew he was far from the help of the forest. In fact, he was far more scared here among the boarded-up buildings and sprawling concrete fields. The sun had just set as Snowflake slowed down and waited for Dolby to catch up. The deer walked up to an unmarked, plain-looking, one-story facility and ducked around the back. "Why are we even here?" Dolby panted. He was exhausted from both a very emotional day, and a very long run, and just wanted to go home and go to bed to forget about it all. He cautiously peered around back but did not see Snowflake. He did, however, see a cracked parking lot with weeds growing up through the asphalt, and a trash dumpster. Figuring

Snowflake was back to her games, he walked quickly toward the dumpster. "I'm not in the mood for Hide-n-seek!"

A deep voice echoed from behind the dumpster.

"Me neither." Dolby stopped in his tracks and backed away, keeping his eyes on the dumpster. Darkness had set in, and the only light behind the building was a dim floodlight whose bulb seemed like it was fifty years old. Dolby jumped at the sound of a bang on the metal receptacle, and then again when the silhouette of a large figure emerged. He continued to back away when the voice yelled, "DOUGH-BOY!" All Dolby could think about was laughing at Steele back in the exam room with his fingers buried you know where, and here he was—alone with him in an abandoned lot. "COME HERE! I've got something to show you." Dolby continued backing up and was about to make a run for it when two hands stopped his momentum from behind. He jumped again.

"Give him a chance. Listen to what he has to say." It was Adele! Steele continued his urgings.

"I'm not gonna hurt you, loser. I have a secret that I want you to see. I've never shown this to anyone, except for a couple of the guys. Promise you will keep this between us?"

"Of course, we will," Adele answered for the both of them, pushing Dolby toward the bully. After looking around to make sure they were alone, with two hands Steele bench-pressed the lid of the dumpster up and tossed it over so that it loudly clanged against the other side. "You're not gonna believe this!" Steele reached in, fished around for a while, and came out holding an item above his head like it was a prized large-mouth bass. "JACKPOT!" he cried. Adele and Dolby were confused to watch him tear into a family-size bag of Nacho Cheese Doritos. "Hep yo-sef!" he mumbled with a mouth full of chips. They stepped over to the dumpster to find snack bags of all sizes and varieties piled to the top. Before making their selection, Dolby had to know more information.

"What is this?"

Steele swallowed. "Only the best place in Gomer! It's a Frito-Lay Distributor. We found this two years ago. When their chips age past the 'eat-by' date, they throw them out. It's some kind of regulation, but the chips are still good. This one says it's only three days past its shelf life. Like I said, this is not for anyone else to know. That way, we get all the chips we want whenever we want them! Be careful, though. They don't like it when they catch you dumpster-diving during the day. Believe me, I know." Frito Corn Chips for dinner did sound good right about now. Adele snatched two snack-sized bags of Rold Gold pretzels. They munched in silence, except for a periodic, "Mmmmm." It kind of felt like Christmas morning to the two sixth graders.

Dolby found a box of Cracker Jack and yelled, "Awesome!" He ripped open the top, dug for the prize at the bottom, and wondered what this secret had to do with what he had just been through. "Hey Steele—what does this have to do with pit bulls and deer?"

Steele was now crunching on some Funyuns. "Nothing. It's just awesome. Free chips anytime you want." Dolby saw through his answer. This was Steele's way of saying he was sorry. Dolby knew he would never actually say it. Dolby accepted his apology by helping himself to some Sun Chips.

Adele piped up. "Actually, Steele does have something else he wanted to show you, right Steele?"

"Oh yeah," Steele said. "But, it also has to be kept between us. The police can't get involved. If they do, it could ruin Dad's business and then he'll go right back to drinking. I know he will. And when he gets drunk, he . . ." The eighth grader stopped himself. "Can we just try and figure this out ourselves?" They agreed. He pulled a folded-up piece of paper from his back pocket and handed it to Dolby. It was stained orange with Cheeto's fingerprints. Dolby stared at a list of dates and numbers and weights.

"I don't get it."

"My dad keeps a record of all the dogs we rehab, and all the clients who adopt them—not too careful, though—he doesn't want to know too much. He doesn't track names, addresses, emails, or phone numbers in case the logbook gets in the wrong hands. I went through the ledger and found something interesting. One of his clients jumped off of the page. He adopts two or three dogs per year—more than any other client. He—his customer number is 0696—also adopts a certain type of pit bull. That's the column on the far right."

Dolby read down the list, "fifty-five pounds, sixty-five pounds, sixty-two pounds, fifty-nine pounds, fifty-two pounds, etcetera."

"That's the weight of the pit bull he is adopting."

"So?" added Adele

"So, those are the largest pit bulls that come through our doors. 0696 is only interested in the biggest and strongest animals we got. Remember how you asked me if we are breeding pit bull terriers?"

"Yeah?" replied Dolby.

"Maybe this is your guy."

"Steele, tell Dolby about the other thing," Adele and Steele had been talking.

"I matched the surveillance camera footage with the dates and times that 0696 took a dog, and he drives a gray El Camino." Dolby shot a look at Adele. "Why are you looking for a dog breeder anyway?" Steele asked innocently. It was now Dolby's turn to tell a few secrets—Steele already knew about his power of speech with deer, and Dolby made the call on the spot that Steele could be of some help. He had forgotten for a second about his mistake of trusting Dell.

Dolby and Adele told Steele everything. Adele even had news for Dolby—she had videotaped a lot of footage after the fire that may also be of some help. They made plans to meet at the Dew Drop Inn after school to watch the tape. The three gathered up all the empty chip bags and labored to stand up, feeling like fattened rats after a county fair. While saying their goodbyes, Steele exclaimed out of habit, "Later Dough-bo . . ." He caught himself but realized that he had called him Dough-boy for so long, that he didn't even remember his real name. He was embarrassed to have to ask what his first name was. Adele read his mind and came to the rescue.

"His name is Dolby."

"You know what? That's okay," said Dolby with a smile. "It doesn't bother me anymore. I know who I am now. You should just keep calling me that—it wouldn't be the same otherwise."

29

VIDEO

"What other dungeon is so dark as one's own heart!"

—*Nathaniel Hawthorne in The House of the Seven Gables (1851)*

Three bicycles laid in a heap by the front door of what could be called an underground railroad for injured and abused pit bull terriers. The odd trio was holed up in what felt like a dungeon in the basement. It was an old coal cellar complete with a hard, dirt floor that was chosen for its privacy. Steele had dragged three camp chairs and an old TV into the makeshift control room. He placed the television in the opening in the wall that was once used as a coal chute to heat the house before it was converted into a hotel. A generator was humming which provided power for what Geema affectionately called the idiot box. Only this idiot box was about to make geniuses of three school kids. Adele shivered from the cold cellar as she connected the video camera's white audio and yellow video cables. Steele threw a bag of popcorn at Dolby, a bag of Lay's at Adele, and kept a bag of Tostito's for himself. Of course, they had biked to the Dew Drop Inn by way of the Frito-Lay distributor and helped themselves even though it was broad daylight. She pushed play with a greasy finger, and the footage began just as the fight between the animals was ending. No video of the fighting was caught on tape, however, because it all occurred inside the segment walled-in by flames. The next thing that is heard on the tape is a loud howl from off-screen, and then after a brief pause, the splashing of the remaining wolf monsters obediently parading back up Cedar Creek single-file. Two more howls are heard as the camera followed the beasts until all seventy or eighty of them were out of view. The camera panned back for one last view of the entire woodscape and then promptly went black.

"Whoa!" cried Steele, "What in the . . ." He caught himself. "I mean, what are those things?!"

"Those are why we are so interested in your breeding history. Somebody who really knows their stuff has combined wolves and coyotes and pit-bulls to form a new species of monster. We think they are coming for all the deer in Gomer next." Dolby continued. "What we know is whoever is behind the attacks has trained them to respond to a high-pitched alarm, and they seem to obey every time. When called, they travel up the creek to a location determined by a smaller Pitcoywolf who wears something like a GPS tracking device. The animals form a circle around the sacrificial runt and make their way toward it, destroying and eating everything in its path. When the animals get to the middle dog, both the dog and the tracker are destroyed. This must tip off the villain to then call back the hounds. But, why does it seem like there are no footprints leading to the circle? In past assaults it looked they were just dropped out of the sky."

"I think I know," Steele replied, clearly enjoying being a part of the covert operation. "Rewind the tape. Keep going. All the way to the beginning. There! Stop." Adele paused the video just after the first howling sound. "See how the beasts are already lining up in single-file before getting to the water? Look—they choose not to take a direct straight-line path to the creek, but they zig-zag their way through the thickest part of the brush that butts up against the banks of the water."

"That way, their tracks are hidden from sight and nobody can trace where they are returning," Adele observed. "I'll bet you that the same pattern exists at my pumpkin patch, Turkeytown, and Deer Pass."

Dolby chimed in. "But, thanks to the whistle being used in the daytime, we were able to witness the water run and the direction they were returning. I'm thinking now that it wasn't supposed to happen during the daytime—like maybe the rabid wolf encounter was a coincidence that forced me to use the whistle at the wrong time." Dolby immediately thought of the Windmaster. "I'll bet there was an ambush planned at night, but a random wolf screwed it up."

"So, do you think the plan was to first get rid of all the strongest of the deer, leaving the rest of the herd more vulnerable to an attack at the base camp?"

"Sounds logical to me, Adele," Dolby replied.

"Who would do that? And why? What does he have against the deer?" asked Steele.

"Good question—that's what we've got to find out."

They watched the tape through a few more times, but no other clues were uncovered. It was Adele's idea to watch it one more time in slow motion. After the second howling noise started, but this time low and slow, Dolby yelled, "There!" Adele froze the screen. "Back up a little. Right there!" He pointed at the top corner of the screen. "There's a human figure hiding in the shadows of a cluster of pines. From your angle at the barn, you can just make him out." He was right, somebody was standing on a distant hill watching from far away. When they focused only on the figure, he could be seen raising his head back at the exact same time as the howling noise. It looked the person was howling like a wolf!

"You don't think . . ." Adele slowly asked.

"Yep. We are dealing with a half-tail," replied Dolby. "A half-tail of wolves."

"A what?" Steele wondered.

"You know how I can talk to deer and understand them? Well, this guy apparently can do that with these awful beings. That's how they know when to come, when to leave, and how to follow the plan."

Adele fast-forwarded the tape to the third time the howl was heard. She paused it just in time to reveal the tiny figure howling and motioning with a long stick for the animals to hurry. "Is that a rifle?" asked Steele.

"No—it looks more like a stick to me," countered Dolby. The kids squinted their eyes to get a closer look. Adele saw it first.

"Guys . . . that's no gun or stick. THAT'S A CANE!" All three of them yelled out together—"MRS. KRANTZ???!"

30

SPIES

"Men were indeed more foolish and more cruel than the beasts of the jungle! How fortunate was he who lived in the peace and security of the great forest!"

—*Edgar Rice Burroughs in Tarzan of the Apes (1912)*

"Are we sure it's her? I mean, it could be a cane. But, it could also be a walking stick or a rifle. The video is shot from too far away to be able to tell for sure. We can't even tell if it's a man or woman or even a kid from this distance. Besides, Mrs. Krantz, school secretary, is about a thousand years old." Adele made a good case causing the boys to question themselves. Steele thought for a second.

"Hold that thought—I'll be right back." He returned with a large portable whiteboard, some markers, an eraser, and a tripod flashlight that he sat on the ground. He plugged in the light, leaned the board against the rock wall and went to work. Without saying a word, he began a list. After just a few entries, the other two caught on and took turns shouting out additional bullet points. In just a few short minutes of brainstorming, the whiteboard had eight items scribbled down.

Mrs. K

1. *First to enter principal's office after buck attack—maybe saw D talk to the deer?*

2. *Has access to the library computer—she was Dell all along?*

3. *Has access to Dolby's locker—knows all the school locker combinations*

4. *Saw the skunk episode—watched deer protect D?*

5. *She catches A and D talking in the library and interrupts angrily*

6. *Has had a lot of years to alter the biology of wolves?*

7. *Is herself a half-tail? So, she knows one when she sees one?*

8. *She lives far out-of-town at the mill—right on the creek*

Dolby was the first to speak up. "I don't know—a lot of this is speculation. We don't have any real proof yet. Just look at all those question marks! Although she *is* crazy as a loon, and according to Geema, her husband is quite odd too."

"And is always working on inventing things," added Adele, remembering the fireside chat with Geema.

"If that old bat was posing as Dell all of this time, I'd love to tell her off." Dolby was feeling stupid all over again for falling for the computer trick.

"No! That's the last thing we want." Steele was again enjoying using his street smarts for something positive. "We can't let on that you know who Dell really is. Think about it—we might be able to use the computer messages for our benefit. You've got to continue on as if you still think it's Adele. Once we figure out a plan to defeat this threat, you can give wrong messages that might help us." This made a lot of sense to Adele and Dolby.

"It seems to me that before we do anything, we need to confirm that the mastermind behind all of this is Edith Krantz. But how?" Dolby asked.

"I think it's time to round up the gang for another stake-out. This time, we're going all the way to the mill," answered Adele.

"The mill?" Steele's voice cracked with concern. "I'm not going up there—haven't you heard all those stories about it being haunted?"

"Sure—everybody has. But add those rumors to the list. Wouldn't it make sense for Mrs. Krantz and her husband to spread those stories to keep everyone away from their operation?"

"I guess, but I'm still not going," Steele remarked.

"Are you kidding me? Big, bad, tough, Steele Canis afraid of an old grist mill?! Wait until Gomer Middle School hears about this!" teased Dolby.

"You wouldn't."

"Watch me!" Dolby knew how important Steele's reputation was to him. Steele knew he was stuck.

"All right. But keep your video camera rolling, Adele." They agreed that the sooner they could figure this out, the better. Against Steele's better judgment, tonight was going to be the night provided they could convince some security guards. Steele sloppily added a number nine to the list—"Haunted mill rumors." Then mumbled to no one in particular, "What am I getting myself into?"

Dressed in black from head to toe, the three school kids waited until well past midnight to make the long hike to the Grist Mill. The fact that it was a school night didn't matter to the three—they were in too deep to worry about sleep. If they wanted to get to the mill directly, they could have taken a shortcut north through a bunch of woods. But, the plan was to follow Cedar Creek past the Dew Drop Inn until they either reached the mill or found something between Steele's and the mill that was of interest. That meant that they had to walk along the running water for a few miles west before it turned and headed north. After a few more miles, the old Gomer Mill could be found on the west side of the creek. The mill hadn't been in operation for at least forty years. Back in its heyday, machinery was used to grind grain into enough flour for the surrounding area. As they traveled they wondered if the mill was still in operation—but this time, one that involved animals. Being too far to walk, the kids each were mounted on a buck like military spies scouting out the enemy's camp. Dolby rode Shadow Muzzle, Steele was atop Monster Horn, and Red Velvet carried Adele. Since Dolby and Adele were already experienced in spying from the Dew Drop Inn, they pictured a similar type of operation—camping out on a hill and watching for hours for something to happen. But, this stake-out would be nothing like that one. In fact, they would find out everything they needed to know in a matter of minutes, not hours. The secret agents approached the mill after finding nothing unusual along all the bends of the creek. They turned off of the creek's bank well early of the building, veering left into thick woods in order to see what was at the very back of the property. The covering of the forest opened up into a clearing to their right about 500 yards north of the mill. They all then saw something that made the bucks stop in their tracks. Right there, in full view, was a tunnel made of metal chain-link fencing that extended from the back of the building all the way north into the covering of the forest. The group moved closer and now traveled along the fenced-in tunnel in the same way they followed the creek earlier. After traveling for a distance of four or five football fields, they were staring at another fenced-in area. This one, though, was a square that had to be ten acres by ten acres in size. One look at the open area caused the six to immediately look at one another as if to say, "Do you see what I'm seeing?" The ground inside the pen was completely trampled in the shape of a circle, and there were piles of bones scattered all over the center. At that moment, the wind shifted and blew toward them causing them all to gag at the odor, including the deer whose sense of smell wasn't what it once was. Dolby saw the source of the stink first and whispered, "Look—there's a pile of rotting meat in the middle."

Adele shook her head and added, "Guys . . . I think it's about to be feeding time." The six hid behind a grove of pine trees upwind, and Adele set up her tripod quietly. Dolby looked at his watch—it was two in the morning. It wasn't five minutes later, that Shadow, Monster Horn and Red all rotated their ears at the same time. The familiar signal had been sounded. Shadow Muzzle's low voice broke the silence.

"Brace yourselves. Here they come!"

31

CREEK

"There is a stream there, I know, black and strong which crosses the path. That you should neither drink of, nor bathe in; for I have heard that it carries enchantment and great drowsiness and forgetfulness."

—*J.R.R. Tolkien in The Hobbit (1937)*

They had all seen the violent rage of the animals before. They had even seen it up close. But, back at the tree fort, they were too busy just trying to survive the flames and the demon dogs to be able to truly take in the utter brutality of the beasts. They were about to witness, without interruption, the true horror of the Pitcoywolves. The growling and howling intensified as they tore single-file through the metal tunnel. One poor creature led the way—it was smaller than the rest, probably a runt of the litter that Mrs. Krantz didn't mind sacrificing. It had a leather collar around its neck with a metal medallion that dangled and swung with each gallop. It looked like a small gold medal, but with a blinking, red light in the center. Dolby thought that this must be the tracker system used by the humans to lead the dog to the predetermined location—maybe with a built-in shocking system like used in an electric dog fence? He also thought rightly that its final destruction and loss of signal probably alerted the person tracking the activity to know when to call back the wolf pack. As they watched and filmed, they were not looking forward to the next scene. The runt Pitcoywolf, about the size of a large pit bull but half the size of the others, sprinted out of the tunnel opening into the large pen. It galloped straight to the center, where it began going to town on the massive pile of meat. The first thirty or forty of the animals did not follow the lead dog, and instead ran to the right, forming a half circle. The rest of the snarling brutes formed the other half of the circle by sprinting to the left. When the front-running Pitcoywolves met at the far end, and the runt was completely surrounded, the creatures turned as one and began racing toward the food in the middle. This was obviously trained behavior in order to exact the most damage. Adele watched a raccoon, who happened to be in the wrong place at the wrong time, get scooped up by the massive jaws of a monster wolf and swallowed whole—all without the animal breaking stride.

"Look! The one in the middle has no clue what is about to—UGH." Steele had to look away—a baby opossum who had earlier ventured into the ring met a quick end. He was right. The runt of the litter was focused only on scarfing down as much food as possible from the center pile and was oblivious to the approaching cannibals. Then they all had to look away when the circle closed in on the food and the lone wolf. The animals were so desperately tearing into the food that it was clear to the spies that part of the strategy was to starve them to increase their ferocity. It was when they saw pieces of metal flying through the air that Shadow, Red, and Monster Horn heard the alarm that was silent to the kids. Surprisingly, the animals quickly obeyed the call and charged to the opening of the tunnel and back toward the mill. They all stared in disbelief—there was nothing left in the middle but a few large bones. They also stared because it was exhausting to watch—the noise, the stress, the smell, the violence. Dolby was far less confident after the carnage he just witnessed.

They stayed hidden for a half of an hour more just to be safe. Adele packed up her video camera, thinking she was done shooting for the night. She would be wrong.

They walked around the other side of the pen and tunnel and noticed a barn tucked away in the distant woods. Adele figured that it must be the breeding facility—an old gray El Camino was parked in front. As they walked toward the back of the mill, they took note that the tunnel had two exits—one toward the feeding pen, and one that emptied into the creek. There was also a crank system to block paths and force animals in the desired direction. The tunnel started at the base of the mill from the double doors of a storm cellar. The animals were being kept underneath the old building, behind cellar doors which also had the same blinking red lights as the collar. They wondered later if it was a security system which unlocked when the collar was activated.

The soothing, quiet sounds of the night had returned, only to be disrupted by a loud, squeaking sound coming from around the front of the wooden structure. "Stay here," Adele whispered to the others, unzipping her camera bag. She found some bushes at the corner of the mill, the creek rushing by on her left. The sound of squeaking continued, which was good because it drowned out the beep made by the record button. She could see an old window slowly being cranked open on the second floor. Below the window spun the large water wheel that was still being powered by the flow of the creek, even though it was of no use anymore. Or was it? A closer look revealed a large, mounted, plastic reservoir that extended from the window down to the top of the spinning paddles of the wheel. At the bottom of the container was a contraption that allowed liquid to drip slowly and continuously over the wheel and into the water. Adele squinted into the viewfinder to see an old man lean out of the window and pour a green liquid out of a large, white bucket into the receptacle. He continued to dump bucket after bucket until the reservoir was full. She watched as a green substance trickled out over the paddle wheels and dripped into the running stream. The window creaked shut. Adele hoped she got a good shot of his face because whatever just happened couldn't be good.

Dolby fired up the library computer for the first time in a long time, not knowing what to expect. After yawning and typing in the password, one lone message popped up on the screen.

```
r u ok
its been awile since we talked
i miss r secret
```

Dolby took a deep breath and typed:

```
                                          ya sorry

          we have bin hangin out so much i 4got to check

                                i will check mor often

                                    i like r secret 2
```

32

ACCIDENT

"In an arm-chair . . . sat the strangest lady I have ever seen, or shall ever see . . . it was then that I began to understand that everything in the room had stopped, like the watch and the clock, a long time ago."

—CHARLES DICKENS IN GREAT EXPECTATIONS (1861)

They were back after school at the vault, as they now called their basement headquarters. Adele manned the controls as usual, and Steele and Dolby directed her when to pause, rewind, and play. The snack of the day was Cool Ranch Doritos as they pored over the film. They were stuck on what Cliff Krantz could be dumping into the water supply of Gomer. "Maybe it's unrelated to any of this and he just enjoys polluting the environment," suggested Adele.

"I don't know—something smells fishy to me," replied Steele. He stuck his nose in the chip bag and inhaled deeply. "Why do some people hate the smell of Cool Ranch Doritos? I looooove how they smell."

"That's it!" cried Dolby. "Follow me, here. Cedar Creek starts in the north and goes all the way south through Gomer. Guess where Cedar Creek flows before hitting town?" He wouldn't wait for an answer. "That's right—Gomer Mill. The water that all the wildlife in the area depend upon to survive is from that creek—it's the only water source. Doesn't it make sense that the reason why all the deer species sense of smell has been compromised is because of something old Cliffy is putting in the water?"

"He did used to be a chemist and work in a lab—before he got fired," added Adele.

"And he's known for being something of an inventor. The collar, the siren, the whistle, the tunnel security system—all could be his work."

Steele began to speak as he added a number ten on the whiteboard. "But why just mess with their smell? I mean, I'm sure he could put something toxic in the water that would just kill them off instantly."

"Yeah, but every other creature would be killed, too. I think they are only targeting deer for some reason. This would make it easier for them to plan an attack without getting detected by scent ahead of time."

"The question I have is why?" Steele said. "I mean, what would make them so obsessed with killing off deer that they would go to all this trouble?" That gave Dolby an idea.

"Hey, Steele, can I use your internet?"

"Sure. Hold on." He returned with a laptop. Dolby opened a search engine and typed, "Gomer Guardian newspaper articles 1960s." It didn't take very long to find out that only articles from 1995 to the present were catalogued online by the Guardian.

"Maybe Geema remembers more. I've got some more questions for her."

"Actually, my dad was picking up a dog in Wanesville today and should be back anytime. Maybe we should meet up later. I think he's gonna want my help."

"Okay, we'll let you know if we find out anything." Adele and Dolby grabbed one more chip for the road.

Dolby and Adele burst into the house through the front door. The kids could tell Geema was in the kitchen from the awful odor that hit them like smelling salts. Dolby groaned—it was liver and onions night. Snowflake was also in the kitchen with both front paws on the counter, snipping asparagus by using one paw to hold down the tip end of the stalk and her mouth to break off the root ends. Dolby loved deer, and Snowflake in particular, but even he could hardly stomach watching one help prepare his food.

"Geema, are you busy?" Dolby asked.

"Honey, I'm never too busy for my sweet grandson."

Dolby felt his face blushing. "Do you remember telling us about Mrs. Krantz and the tragedy that happened to her son?"

"Oh dear. That was forty years ago. I'm not sure I remember much more than what I told you."

"But, it was a car accident that killed him, right?"

"Yes."

"What year was it?"

"Well, let me see. Your mother was a tenth grader at the time. She graduated in 1980. Musta been roundabout 1978—pretty sure it was winter. I remember it happening early in the year. I'm sorry dears, I don't recall any more of the specifics. Only that Edith and Cliff never really recovered. He was their only child and just a baby at age sixteen. I can't even imagine."

"It's just that we have a school project about seatbelt use," he lied, "and it would be great if we could get some more information."

"You could try the library. They may have old Guardian newspapers on file—probably on microfiche."

The juvenile detectives slid their bicycle wheels into the library bike rack. They both stopped in the lobby wondering where the microfiche machines were, and more importantly, *what* they were. "What even is a micro-fish anyway?" asked Adele.

Dolby answered, "Yeah, it sounds like a cool, new deep-sea discovery that you can barely see."

"You're making me want an aquarium full of micro fishes," said Adele.

"SSSSSHHHH," came the scold along with a bonus glare from Mrs. Snodgrass, head librarian at Gomer Public Library. She was among the sweetest women in town, until you broke the rules of her kingdom. Then she became a fire-breathing, four-eyed dragon with bluish-gray hair in a bun. They looked lost, so she had compassion on them. Dolby imagined her breathing out a couple of puffs of smoke as she walked over. Mildred Snodgrass needed to get closer in order to recognize Dolby and whispered, "Dolby Hart, as I live and breathe! Is there something I can help you with?"

"My Geema says . . ." he only got out three words.

"Ohhhhh, how is your dear grandmother? You know we've played some serious Canasta in our day—the two of us!"

"I know," Dolby replied, hoping to get on with the tiny fishing. "She always speaks well of you, Mrs. S., but can you tell us about microfishing?"

Mrs. Snodgrass lowered her head, looked over her bifocals and laughed. "Good one, Mr. Hart! But I wish I could say I'd never heard that one before. At my age, I think I've heard them all. Follow me." She led them to a group of file cabinets in the dusty, backroom archive where nobody ever ventured. Because of that fact, she spoke up. "Well, what exactly are you looking for?"

"Do you have old Guardian newspapers on file?"

"We sure do—all the way back to the 1950s. Ohhhh, the 1950s. Your grandmother and I had such a ball in the fifties—drive-ins, Poodle skirts—those were the days. Let me tell you, when we got all gussied up for the Sock Hops, we would dance . . ."

"That's great," Dolby interrupted. "Where do you keep the microfishes from 1978?"

She scanned the cabinets. "Here we are." She wasn't offended at not being able to finish her story—she had grown used to it. She pulled out a wide drawer, ran her finger along the files, and removed one labeled *1978 Gomer Guardians*. "Do you know what month you are looking for?"

"I guess we need to start in January." She walked them over to the Microfiche Reader. Without explaining anything, they watched her every move, so they could do the research alone. She pulled out a flat, plastic sheet from an envelope which looked like tiny photographs of the pages of a clear newspaper. She pulled a tray from the machine toward her, lifted up what looked like the lid of a copier and placed the microfiche under the lid. She then twisted an assortment of buttons to orient, zoom, and focus the image that now appeared blown up on a monitor that resembled an old computer. Different newspaper articles zoomed through the screen as she moved the tray around. Mrs. Snodgrass jerked her head in the direction of some faraway noisemakers, whispered "SSSSHHHH," and prepared to go on the prowl.

"Can you children take it from here?" They thought she would never ask. Figuring out what they were looking for would be easy to find since it surely would have been front-page news. They checked every headline in January without any luck. As they moved on to February, they began to hope Geema was remembering correctly. They hated the idea of going through the tedious process for ten or eleven more months. But, they wouldn't have to—the article they found next would be all they needed.

"Here it is!" mumbled Adele with a shove of her friend. The eyes of both investigators scanned back and forth in silence as they took in and processed the blurry words they were reading. In bold, black, block letters, the front-page headline next to a black-and-white picture of a sixteen-year old boy, announced,

LOCAL TEEN DIES IN TRAGIC CAR ACCIDENT

The rest of the article read:

> **GOMER**, Joseph Krantz, 16, of Gomer Township passed away last night at Gomer General Hospital from head injuries resulting from an automobile accident on Booger Hollow Road at approximately 10 p.m. on Friday, February 14. Krantz was driving home from a Gomer High School basketball game, where he starred on the court for the past two years. Even though alcohol is not thought to be a factor, it is believed that Krantz was driving too fast on a stretch of road that is often used by local boys as a drag racing track. Nobody else was in the vehicle and no word on whether another driver was involved. However, the blue Buick Skylark was found in the ditch completely totaled with a dead and bloodied eight-point buck discovered nearby, leading local authorities to believe that the ultimate cause of the accident was a whitetail deer leaping in front of the car. Police are continuing the investigation. Krantz is survived by his mother, Edith, and father, Cliff, both of Gomer. Visitation and funeral arrangements are forthcoming.

The words *buck* and *whitetail* leaped off of the screen at Adele and Dolby. "Their son was killed by a whitetail on Valentine's Day!" Dolby shook his head sadly. "There's your motive. That's why they are obsessed with killing the deer in Gomer—they have been plotting revenge for forty years. That's why they're trying to destroy everyone's holidays. If they are going to suffer at each holiday without their only child, then I guess they want others to suffer too." They printed off a copy of the article and headed back to tell Steele. As they walked out to their bikes, Adele summarized their findings.

"I know that must be horrible to go through. But, it just goes to show you, if you stay stuck in the past, it could drive you literally crazy."

Dolby knew that the next few days of messages were going to be crucial. He had to give away information without making it seem like he was giving away information.

                                              gess what

???

                    we figured out wen the next attack will b

???

     valentimes day-1st halloween then thanksgiving then
                         xmas its always on a holiday

So wats the plan then

33

VAULT

"Always mystify, mislead, and surprise the enemy, if possible;
and when you strike and overcome him, never let up in the pursuit so long as
your men have strength to follow; for an army routed, if hotly pursued,
becomes panic-stricken and can then be destroyed by half their number."

—GENERAL STONEWALL JACKSON

The whiteboard in the underground vault now had a hand-drawn calendar next to the list. It was like any other calendar except that it didn't bother to include the first half of January, the last half of February, or any other month for that matter. It only concerned itself with the essential dates. It started with January 25, which was the date the calendar was created, and the date they found out about the probable date of attack. It ended with February 14, which was circled and had a line connecting it to outside the calendar. Next to the line was scribbled, "40th anniversary of Joe's death." Taped to the bottom of the whiteboard was the printout from the 1978 edition of the Guardian. "Just about three weeks until the predicted date of attack—two weeks and six days to be exact." The second he heard what Dolby and Adele found out at the library, Steele went to work with the dry erase markers. "That's all the time we have to come up with a plan and communicate it to the others." In the coming days, the vault would become like a modern-day military war room where Generals and other high-ranking officials strategized their next battle moves. A map of Gomer would be attached to the wall complete with "X's" and lines and arrows in various colors. A poster board, too, would be added with a table of specific times and actions to be carried out. A visitor to the war vault would have no doubt wondered what was indicated by the orange-colored circles that dotted each of the maps and boards. But, these were merely evidence of a love for Frito-Lay Cheetos snacks.

Steele left Adele and Dolby alone while he helped his dad upstairs. Dolby stood at the board, double-checking some timing issues, stopped and mumbled aloud absent-mindedly, "Huh?"

"What is it?" asked Adele.

"Oh nothing."

"Seriously, are our calculations wrong?"

"No, no—nothing like that. I just all of a sudden realized that in just about a year's time, I have gone from contemplating suicide to organizing an operation as a half-tail that has the potential to save both us and the deer population of Gomer. Hard to believe sometimes," stated Dolby.

Adele had never asked anything about his life before moving to Gomer. "Do you mind if I ask you a personal question?"

"I guess?"

"When you were considering suicide, were you serious about it, or was it just, um, like, attention-getting?"

"Hmmmm. Good question. I don't think I would have actually done it. It was more of a sick fantasy—an escape—to get through the pain. I never really thought about the specifics of how I would go through with it. The only specific piece I fantasized about was, if I went through with it, I would be wearing my denim overalls."

"Why? What's the deal with the overalls?"

"A couple of things. First, before I moved to Gomer, I used to wear them all the time—they were my favorite—very comfortable and reminders of happier times. After Steele hung me up by them, I vowed to never wear them again because of how humiliated I felt. But now, as I think about it, I could see myself wearing them at the end as a way to feel close to my mom again. The day she left—the day she said her goodbyes—I was wearing those overalls. I don't think I could ever wear them again unless it was a moment like that. Because, in a weird way, it would be a reminder of her."

Adele didn't respond because they were interrupted by the return of Steele. But, she had to admit that the heavy turn the conversation took did cause her concern. She thought it odd that he still talked of suicide as if it were a present possibility.

They finalized their responsibilities and departed in haste. Each of the three military leaders had their part of the plan to execute separate from the others. Dolby would burn many calories in the coming weeks walking slowly around the Ring of Nod brainstorming, explaining the role of the whitetail in the operation, and giving orders. The map on the large Maple tree, like the one in the vault, was now much more detailed with multiple carvings up and down the trunk. Dolby would also spend many nights seeking wisdom from Geema, being careful not to give away too many details. He knew that too many cooks in the kitchen would spoil the broth. He also knew from experience that it took any cook in the kitchen to spoil liver and onions. Adele spent her time picking the brains of her dad and Officer Robinson. They would have a role in the plan, but only at the end. The police would be kept in the dark for most of the operation so as to not jeopardize both Swampy's business and his recovery from alcoholism. Dolby and Steele felt bad about keeping part of the plan secret from Adele, but they knew it was for the best. If she knew what they had up their sleeves, she would've never signed off on it. They decided it was better for her to be in the dark than either worry her head off at best, or at worst, completely ruin their plan. Steele, for his part, would continue using his street smarts to work on the logistics of the counter-attack. He even sat down to an interview with Mr. Barney Vanderflunder to see if he could find out any more dirt on Mr. and Mrs. Krantz. Mr. V would prove to be very little help, although it was worth it for Steele to get called "Stone" over and over, and also to watch him knock over a lamp onto his office floor.

The operation was well under way. If that same visitor to the vault read the calendar now, he or she would see a large, red circle around February 12 with three large letters underneath—ODP—Operation Deer Preserve.

The way that Dolby was acting lately, one would be surprised to learn how nicely the plan was coming together. By now, the operation was all that was on his mind. But, the more he thought about the details, the more saddened he became. First of all, his friends, both no-tail and whitetail, were going to be risking their lives on the night of February 12th. That was a scary proposition for Dolby—he had never had friends that he cared about before. They knew that they could not fight army against army. If they waged a straight-up battle, there would be far too many casualties and no guarantee of victory. There were still up to eighty grizzly monsters remaining against about twenty fighting stags. The odds were not in their favor. The only other way was to follow through with the strategy that put many of them in harm's way. He knew it was the only way, but it still made him nervous.

So wats the plan then

                                              no plan
???

        after seeing the big creetures the deer r just
                              escaping gomer
seriously

                                                  yep
wen

                         they r evacuating b4 the 14th
Do u know wen

                              the nite of the 12th
wat time

                                         @ midnight
where r they going

                    east along the creek toward glendale

                              but im worried
???

   most of the bucks from far away r leaving earlier in
                the day so the herd will b defense less

im sure itll b fine they only have 2 get out of gomer
& away from the big dogs

                                           i gess
1 night of traveling & they will b safe

Mrs. Krantz now knew the night and time to send out her monster wolves if she wanted to attack the vulnerable herd. Dolby wiped the palm sweat off of the computer mouse with a Kleenex. He knew there was nothing more to do. The bait was set—he hoped she would take it.

34

OPERATION

"We shall go on to the end . . . we shall fight on the seas and oceans, we shall fight . . . in the air . . . we shall fight on the beaches . . . we shall fight in the fields and on the streets, we shall fight in the hills, we shall never surrender."

—*BRITISH PRIME MINISTER WINSTON CHURCHILL*
(JUNE 4, 1940)

February 12

Everyone was in position for Operation Deer Preserve. All involved had been briefed on what to do and when. All they could do now was wait and hope that Cliff and Edith Krantz took the bait and moved their attack date up a couple of days. If not, plan B was to assemble each night until they mounted their final onslaught. If nothing happened through February 14, they would just have to go back to the drawing board. Dolby and Shadow Muzzle were posted at the Brown's farm with Dolby fifty feet up in the air observing on the old rusty steps of a grain silo. Shadow was at the foot of the silo ready to take off when the time came. Dolby looked at his watch.

11:30 p.m.

He could see under the moonlight that Steele, Monster Horn, Canuck, and Gus and a dozen other bucks had taken their stations near the creek.

Snowflake, too, was positioned to make an important contribution. They all were well-hidden in thickets up and down the banks of the flowing water. The four bucks and Steele were the first to be thrown into danger and they waited with hearts racing from adrenaline. Adele would join them later at the Grist Mill with Officer Robinson and Chief Kowalski—if everything was executed according to plan.

11:45 p.m.

Dolby had heard the phrase, "There are no atheists in foxholes." He knew that it referred to the fact that human beings are hard-wired by their Creator to know that He exists, which bubbles to the surface when facing life-or-death situations. He nervously laughed to himself that he was the atheist in the foxhole about to pray. He kept hearing Fantasma's words in his mind—"The answer to all is the Windmaster," and, "The Master of the winds is out to get you, but not how you think." So, there in his fox hole fifty feet in the air, Dolby prayed for his friends and for a successful next few hours. The team of middle schoolers figured that if wolves ran at a top speed of thirty-five miles per hour, then bigger and stronger Pitcoywolves would probably run between forty-five and fifty-five mph—as fast as a horse. They calculated that the distance along the winding, L-shaped creek from the mill north of town to east of base camp was fifteen miles. So, they estimated that it would take the monster dogs about twenty minutes to get to the area where Mrs. Krantz thinks the evacuation of the deer will be taking place. But, their plan called for the runt with the GPS shock collar to be intercepted by a dozen bucks closer to the Brown's farm, which is about ten miles as the creek flows. Accounting for the Pitcoywolves not being able to run at full speed, they forecasted the runt to arrive at around thirteen minutes after the siren sounded. Once the runt arrived, they knew the rest of the pack wouldn't be far behind. Mr. and Mrs. Krantz themselves had to time things so that the full-sized creatures didn't overtake the lead wolf before it got to the desired location. Dolby thought that once the runt hit the Brown's, they would have about seven minutes before the rest showed up. Based on all of that, if the Krantz's were attacking tonight, they should be hearing an alarm in the next five to ten minutes.

11:50 p.m.

It may have been the longest five minutes of Dolby's young life, especially since the alarm is silent to his ears. He was constantly watching Shadow for a reaction. As he also scanned the moonlit forest and all the animals at their posts, he began to fear that all of the planning and lack of sleep was for nothing. What if Mrs. K saw through his computer lies? What if she had schemed a different plan than the one they all hoped for? He whispered a phrase to himself, "The answer to all is the Windmaster." He suddenly felt that even if this night didn't turn out like he wanted that there was another blast of wind to discover, and that it would all work out in the end. Sure enough, Dolby watched Shadow's ears rotate quickly, followed by a jerk of his head toward him. "The alarm has sounded young half-tail! The alarm has sounded!"

12:08 a.m.

Correction—the next eighteen minutes would be the longest of Dolby's life. He thought it would be thirteen minutes before catching sight and sound of the runt. But, he underestimated. He started to doubt himself again when he heard it—a loud splashing sound coming from the distant west. He focused his binoculars and sure enough, a smaller, wolf-sized Pitcoywolf wildly sprinted down the creek toward them. Dolby grunted a loud "GET READY!" to the nearby bucks and shined his flashlight in Steele's direction. He watched as they all tensed up and stared forward like lions ready to spring from tall grass. Monster Horn was on the south side of the creek, while Canuck, Gus, and Red Velvet were on the north side. As the splashing got louder, Monster Horn kept his eyes locked on to Red Velvet—who had a better view—for a sign. At the correct moment, Red stomped on the ground and Monster Horn leaped out of the brush and into the stream right in the path of the oncoming wolf. This action startled the wolf so that it instinctively leaped at the buck with fangs ready to bite and tear. At its highest point, Monster Horn lowered his head and in one motion, caught the beast in its antlers and tossed it onto the bank across from where he started. The creature had no chance to escape because the second it thudded to the ground, three bucks pinned it to the earth. Even though trapped, the beast struggled to wriggle free, but its strength was no match for the elk, Red Deer, and Mule Deer. Canuck immobilized the animals back end, while Gus pressed down on its torso. Red had the hardest job of attempting to keep its head from moving as the snarling beast violently snapped its jaws behind the cage of spikes. Monster Horn jumped in to add his horns to the cage. They both adjusted their racks so that the animal could no longer move its jaws and head. At that point, Steele moved in. As he went to reach around the antlers of the bucks, he suddenly froze as his mind flashed-back to the moment in the principal's office when he was the one behind the cage. The grunt of the bucks snapped him out of it. Despite gagging at the smell of its breath, Steele skillfully unbuckled the collar, and quickly tossed it to Snowflake, who caught it in her mouth. Snowflake wasted no time, sprang into the water and sprinted away through the creek, taking the signal toward the pretend evacuation spot. This was done to buy time and keep the Krantz's thinking that all was well from their end of things. Steele hoped that whoever was monitoring the progress of the collar would not notice the slower pace of the doe. Snowflake was flanked by two guards on each side of the creek—Saluja, the Sambar Buck and Wapiti, the Tule Elk, who both galloped at the same speed as the young doe.

Meanwhile, Dolby watched from high atop the silo. The baying and snarling of the runt wolf soon stopped and the creature now laid motion-less on the bank of the creek. Once he received the return flashlight signal from Steele, he tore down the metal ladder and jumped onto the back of Shadow Muzzle. He had no time to lose. They had to get to the mill be-fore the oncoming demon dogs arrived at their current location near the Brown's property. According to his calculations, he had about seven min-utes to travel the one-mile straight-line route north through the woods to the mill. The remaining bucks made a half-circle blockade around Cedar Creek, preparing for a possible battle. It all depended on Shadow Muzzle and Dolby's race to the pen behind the Gomer Mill.

35

RUNT

"They began to drag the bound and muzzled Lion to the Stone Table . . .
once Aslan had been tied on the flat stone, a hush fell over the crowd . . .
The children did not see the actual moment of the killing.
They couldn't bear to look and had covered their eyes."

—C.S. Lewis in
The Lion, the Witch and the Wardrobe (1950)

12:11 a.m.

Dolby looked at his watch, thankful at how fast Shadow had navigated the dark forest. The stag lowered Dolby to the ground near the chain-link fence tunnel. Dolby made sure the tunnel was open at the entrance of the creek. He then turned the crank in order to block the way back toward the cellar. He placed a large rock behind it to keep it in place. This ensured that the only path the Pitcoywolves could go was down the long tunnel and into the pen, and not back under the mill. Dolby shoved his hand into his right pocket to check once again—it was still there. He hopped back onto Shadow who followed the fence tunnel to where it emptied into the pen. He asked Shadow to walk him over to a hedge of blackberry bushes to check if another item was still in place—it was. Shadow carried the boy to the enclosure, lowering him down inside. Shadow knew he should leave, but he couldn't pull himself away. He hugged him with his neck and whispered in a low voice, "Dolby good half-tail." The half-tail fought back tears as he turned toward the center. Dolby realized as he took his place that once again, he was the runt of the litter. All he could do now was listen and wait.

12:15 a.m.

Mortimer the Moose was posted down river closer to town about a mile west of the Brown's. He was perched on an elevation that overlooked a curve in the creek. His only job was to keep watch for the Pitcoywolves as they barreled around the bend, and then alert Dolby when they had made it that far. It was habit to raise his wide, brown nose into the air for clues, but of course, he could not detect a thing. He wouldn't need his sense of smell. The night was quickly filled with the howls and growls of an army of frantic monster wolves that were racing their way, some in single file, and others running two-by-two. The wolves had whipped themselves into such a frenzy of madness, that they even snapped their jaws at each other. All 1500 pounds of the massive moose shuddered at the scene. Mortimer focused on the job at hand and waited for the proper moment. His position was above the widest part of Cedar Creek which would be the ideal place for what would happen next. When the mass of violence was about a football field before the wide spot, Mortimer lifted his nose up into the air again, but this time to signal Dolby. He proceeded to use all of his massive frame to bugle as loudly as he could through the night air. In just mere seconds, his call was answered with another call—Dolby's treehouse whistle. The thirty seconds of sound surprisingly carried well through the clear night. Mortimer watched as the lead demon took the bait and slowed down in his tracks just as the water flowed wider. The rest of the creatures followed suit until all eighty of them had somehow turned around and changed course. They had heard the signal to return to the mill! They retraced their previous steps and in no time, were now stampeding in the opposite direction back toward Gomer Mill. Mortimer trumpeted out another long bellow to indicate that the whistle had been heard by the approaching herd. The moose shuddered again at the sight of the once clear brook now tinted dark and red with the blood of bitten Pitcoywolves.

12:20 a.m.

Snowflake decided it was time to veer off course from the creek to test the electric collar. It was still in her mouth, so she was not looking forward to the shock. The second she departed from the line of the water, she felt a stunning jolt between his teeth. Sprinting forward and kicking water up, she expected to be stunned away from the water and toward the desired location of the Krantz's. Snowflake jerked when it happened and obeyed the collar's guidance faithfully until it stopped her in the middle of an open field—the exact place Dolby had revealed to Dell. Snowflake couldn't get rid of that electric zapper fast enough. She tossed it down onto a flat rock and proceeded to get her revenge by stomping it into little bits. This, of course, was what the Krantz's were waiting for. Once they saw that the signal was destroyed, they knew the damage had been done. The deer had all been destroyed, and they had finally avenged a forty-year grudge born of pain and suffering. They had gotten their revenge. It may not have been the exact anniversary of the whitetail stealing their Joseph from them, but the final retaliation was still just as sweet. Snowflake heard the second Krantz alarm calling the dogs back home, somehow found a second wind, and began his trek back to the mill.

12:23 a.m.

Dolby nervously fingered the whistle deep in his pocket and chuckled to himself at the irony that the whistle given by Mrs. Krantz designed to destroy the whitetail, was hopefully to spell her doom. The silence of the moment gave the boy a brief opportunity to take stock in the last six months of his life. Dolby Hart, of all people, the laughingstock of the sixth grade, was chosen to be the half-tail hero of a generation of white-tailed deer. At least he hoped that would be his legacy. He remembered how important he felt at the Ring of Nod; how much respect he was given by great buck warriors; how much he learned from Fantasma Bianca, the Phantom of the Wood. Mostly, he thought about the Windmaster. He nervously chuckled to himself when he realized his life was actually flashing before his eyes. Even though he didn't pretend to understand why the winds blew as they did in his life, he now trusted the strength and direction of those invisible winds. And as if on cue, a cool, refreshing, pleasant, pine-smelling breeze blew out of the south and enveloped Dolby. He still feared what was coming, but he faced it in the strength and confidence that he was not alone. With eyes closed, Dolby basked in that peaceful joy for many minutes and couldn't help feeling like maybe the Master of the Winds had gotten him after all.

Just then, the hooves of Monster Horn rhythmically came to a halt by the blackberry bushes. Steele jumped down from the buck's back and began dragging something from the bushes. It was a steel plate that he leaned against the outside of the tunnel.

12:28 a.m.

The arrival of the Pitcoywolves was unmistakable. They splashed into the metal tunnel in a wild frenzy as if someone just took away their dinner. Desperate for meat, the beasts slammed into each other and the fencing as they charged forward toward Dolby and the open pen. The hysterical creatures with fangs bared were too much for Dolby to watch so he closed his eyes and let his sense of hearing tell the story. First, he heard the parade of demons circling around both sides and behind him. He decided they must all be in circular formation because the next thing he heard was the loud clang of Steele blocking the exit with the steel plate. They were now trapped inside the pen, along with Dolby, with nowhere to go. The rush of the beasts now turned in his direction sounded like hell had unleashed its worst on him. For some reason, the scene seemed to slow down for Dolby as he heard another commotion. For him to hear it over the wild snapping of the dogs meant that whatever was happening had to have been mighty loud—it was the hysterical screaming of Adele.

12:30 a.m.

Adele couldn't wait any longer and showed up to the arena a good half of an hour earlier than was rehearsed. She never imagined the nightmare of a scene that played out in front of her. What followed next was the part of the plan that Dolby and Steele kept from her. She saw the wolves charging and could not believe her eyes. They were charging at a helpless Dolby! She screamed and sprinted toward the pen where Steele held the plate in place. Her screams escalated when she got a closer look at Dolby—he was wearing overalls! He was wearing the exact same overalls that he said made him feel close to his mom; the same overalls which Dolby all but called his suicide outfit. She wailed "NOOOO!" over and over as she joined the wolves in

149

charging forward. Steele turned around in time to stop her. He grabbed the little farm girl by the shoulders and effortlessly pushed her down.

"STAY BACK—IT'S THE ONLY WAY!" he yelled.

On the ground, feelings of hatred and betrayal took control of Adele. Memories of all the times Steele humiliated and harmed Dolby flooded her mind. "I KNEW IT—YOU WERE NEVER OUR FRIEND! YOU SET HIM UP ONCE AND FOR ALL! I HATE YOU!" She got up and flailed her arms wildly as she hit him over and over. Steele easily overpowered her and held her still with both hands, forcing her to watch with him Dolby's fate.

12:31 a.m.

Dolby knew it was time to face the howling music. He opened his eyes just in time to see the teeth and red eyes of five crazed monsters leaping toward him in the air. Bracing himself, he gagged on their rotten breath, and felt warm saliva slap against his face. Just before the moment of impact, Dolby's loud cry echoed eerily through the Gomer woods. Adele watched with horror as her best friend willingly sacrifices himself in order to trap the beasts and save his deer friends.

36

DEFEAT

"And behold, every Philistine's sword was against his fellow,
and there was very great confusion."

—1 *Samuel 14:20*

12:32 a.m.

Adele's screams mixed with Dolby's. From her vantage point on the ground, she watched as Dolby disappeared behind a blur of blackness. The bear-sized animals now blocked him completely from view. By this time, the tears streaming from her eyes made the scene hazy. It looked a lot like circling lions devouring a fresh kill on the African Sahara. She was about to turn away in despair when Dolby suddenly appeared in her sights again. This made her stand up at attention to get a closer look. Her heart was beating through her chest. The body of Dolby Hart flew airborne above the raging demons, like a piece of meat tossed over the snapping jaws of a river of alligators. She screamed "NOOOOOO!" once more, awaiting Dolby's return to earth, and the inevitable ripping apart of her friend like a rag doll. Only, the return didn't occur—almost like the law of gravity failed at the most opportune time! Adele's breath quickened, her eyes bulged, and she watched Dolby being lifted up from the ground higher and higher and out of danger!

The yell that Adele heard previous to the aerial rescue wasn't due to fear on the part of Dolby. It had been a premeditated, loud grunt, and Monster Horn and Shadow Muzzle were awaiting the signal. It was a cry of "NOW!" in their own language. At that moment, the two bucks, who were stationed under a massive tree nearby, lowered their racks, ran away from the pen, and pulled. A steel cable attached to the antlers of the deer extended up and over a branch and yanked the boy up into the air, just as the jaws of the beasts were clamping down. Dolby ascended upward by the other end of the cable which was attached to the shoulder straps of his denim overalls. HALF-TAIL WAS RISING! Dolby continued to ascend skyward above the murderous mayhem below! The wolves leaped and snapped their jaws, biting only air. He was now dangling in the air above the chaos. He had an all-too intimate seat at what would come next. The five Pitcoywolves to get to Dolby first were now jumping and snapping with anger and violence below him. Their frustration and hunger spilled over, causing them to begin to bite and attack each other. It was all happening very quickly, but also according to plan. The first five animals were now fighting each other to the death, while other black figures joined the brawl until it became a free-for-all just below the feet of the hanging boy. His overalls now splattered with blood, Dolby prayed that the cable would hold. The center ground of the pen turned dark with black and red as fangs ripped and tore flesh and bone. The demonic sounds and putrid smells horrified Dolby and would become the source of nightmares for months to come. The death-match below continued but became less intense as more and more monsters lost the fight. The strongest and largest of the creatures remained active in wildly consuming what used to be their partners in crime. By this time, all of the fighting stags were surrounding the outside of the enclosure, waiting for the signal. Just four savages remained frantically feeding in four separate piles. Shadow knew it was time to act. At his loud wheeze, twenty bucks leaped over the fence and into the fray. They divided themselves up into groups of four and five to take on each remaining monster. With four or five deer against every one Pitcoywolf, the surviving animals didn't survive very much longer.

1 2 : 4 5 a.m.

Dolby didn't care how awkward he looked suspended in mid-air pumping his fists, kicking his legs, and celebrating. He fought back tears of joy to think that he had played a major role in saving his friends, and that months of investigating and planning and rehearsing had proven successful. He had been suspended by his suspenders before, but this time, he didn't care who saw him up there, or how long he stayed swinging in the breeze. Dolby then felt the velvety flat and broad surface of Mortimer Moose's rack support him mid-air as Shadow and Monster slowly lowered him down. The moose and the rest of the deer then paraded around the perimeter in a victory lap, with Mortimer carrying Dolby in the front. Loud bugles, bellows, snorts, bleats and other noises of approval filled the air as the half-tail hero was elevated for all to see.

It was at that moment that others did arrive to see. Mr. and Mrs. Krantz, no doubt hearing the uproar, sped up in their gray El Camino and skidded to a slushy halt. Mrs. Krantz jumped out of the passenger side wailing at the sight of her precious creations all dead in a heap. "MY BABIES!" she screamed over and over. "WHAT HAVE YOU DONE TO MY BABIES?!"

The next car to pull up sported blue and red lights swirling on the hood. Officers Robinson and Kowalski, along with Clayton Brown and Jed Calhoun, all got out of the car to see if everything that Adele had told them was true. The policemen's first move was to pull Cliff Krantz from the driver's seat of his car, yank his arms behind his back, and clamp shut a pair of handcuffs. "You are under arrest for the environmental crime of dumping hazardous waste with intent to harm wildlife." Officer Robinson had seen the footage and had Gomer's water supply tested—both were proof enough to put Cliff behind bars for quite a while. While he was being deposited in the backseat of the squad car, Mrs. Krantz, too, was being pushed with hands behind her back to join her husband.

The two cops left the back door of the car open as they stood guard comparing notes and discussing protocol. So engrossed were they in the conversation, that they did not notice a small critter shuffling under their noses toward the criminals sitting in the car. A black-and-white-striped-mammal boldly approached the Krantz's, made a quick 180-degree spin, lifted up her tail, and doused the couple with an offensive, sulfur-smelling anal gland concoction. Stinkerbelle had struck again!

37

GOODBYES

"He makes my feet like the feet of deer; he enables me to stand on the heights."

—*PSALM 18:33*

Three Weeks Later

In just three short weeks, life had gotten back to normal since the success of Operation Deer Preserve. For Dolby, that wasn't necessarily a good thing. Now that there was no longer any threat to the deer population, Dolby's role as half-tail was no longer needed. He had settled back into the boring routine of school, homework, and being the class doormat again. Without a reason to meet, Steele and Adele no longer had any time for him. Whenever he asked them to hang out, they always offered a different excuse. Even Snowflake wasn't around much these days—she spent all of her time at what used to be base camp helping the rest of the whitetail tear down and pack up. At least he still had Geema. She finished cleaning up the Saturday morning pancake dishes and plopped down in front of the fireplace to catch up on some knitting. Dolby laid on his stomach on the family room floor with a history textbook open in front of him. "Are you okay, honey?" Geema finally asked. She hadn't seen a page turn in fifteen minutes.

"Yeah—I'm just tired." It wasn't completely a lie—Geema's chocolate chip pancakes always gave him a food coma.

"Are you sure, dear? You've been awfully quiet these last few days."

"I don't know," Dolby replied, "I guess it's just a lot of things. Things at school haven't changed—it's hard going from a celebrated half-tail to a no-body overnight." Adele, Steele and Dolby had kept Geema up many nights with stories about their exploits. "My friends don't have time for me, the deer are moving out, and . . ." He caught himself before sharing what was really on his mind. But, Geema wouldn't let him get away with it.

"And?"

"I just . . . I want . . . I don't know." He collapsed face first into the old, orange shag carpet. Geema knew enough to give him time to collect his thoughts. He lifted up his head. "I guess I wish that Mom could have seen me, or at least been around so I could tell her about it all." Despite his head going down again, she knew he wasn't done. Up it came again. "I guess I don't understand why Adele gets to have her mom and dad, while both of my parents left me." Geema had more information she wished she could share. Instead, she told Dolby to look up.

"What do you see right now?"

"Um, you."

"What else?"

"Uh . . . a rocking chair and a fireplace?"

"No—in my hands."

"A needle and yarn."

"No, right *here*." She held up her needlepoint with both hands. She was almost finished with a cross-stitching of a horse she planned to frame for her sister's birthday. "What do you see?" He was looking up at the backside of the embroidery.

"Well, I see different random colors, ugly patterns, hanging thread—basically a jumbled mess. Why?"

Geema pressed him further. "Is it very beautiful?"

"You know it's not. It's pretty stinkin' ugly and doesn't make a lot of sense."

"Exactly," Geema had gotten the answer she wanted. "But guess what? From where I sit, looking at it from the front side, it makes perfect sense. It's beautiful and a masterpiece thanks to whoever designed it. Our lives are like this needlework. It may look messy and ugly from our perspective, but we have to trust that a Designer is not finished with His handiwork yet. From the other side, it's beautiful, is a work of art, and makes perfect sense. Only we aren't able to see what the Creator is designing until we see it from the other side. God is not done with your masterpiece, Dolby. Your job is to trust that whatever He's doing is so good that you wouldn't change one thing if you saw what He saw and knew what He knew." That took some time to process for Dolby. By this time, he was now sitting up, staring into the fire.

"Geema?

"Yes, dear?"

Dolby was thinking of the phrase, *the Windmaster is out to get you.* "Do you think God pursues people? I mean, does He work in their lives trying to get their attention? Through this whole experience, I keep getting the feeling that He is out to get me—but, in a good way."

"Oh sure, sweetie. Back in my day, folks would call Him the *Hound of Heaven* for that very reason. The way the bible says it, Jesus came to seek and save the lost."

Dolby had certainly felt lost for a long time. But, he had one last question. "Then how does a person know if He is chasing after them?"

Geema thought for a second. "Oh honey, that's an easy one. There's a simple way to tell if He's chasing you down, and that is . . ." Geema paused for effect, ". . . if you want to be caught."

Later that morning, Dolby was glad to see his old friend Snowflake walk into the house. She was by this time over a hundred pounds, and much too big to be a house pet, but they didn't care. She greeted Geema first with a lick on the cheek, and then asked Dolby if he wanted to head to base camp with her. Dolby excitedly looked at his Grandma, who knew her grandson too well and responded with a nod and a smile. "Just be home before dark, you two."

It was odd for Dolby to walk up the path to base camp and not see sentry deer guarding the hill. There were broken barricades scattered across the hill that were fallen and in need of repair. Even the entrance to the camp was now wide open without the need of a password, or more accurately, a pass-stomp. The deer population at the camp was clearly sparser than before. One-by-one, whitetail, blacktail, red deer, elk, moose and caribou bowed before Dolby as they left Gomer to begin their long journeys to distant homes in distant lands. Those closest to Dolby stopped and said a few words of goodbye. "Well, it's been a real hoot-n-a-holler!" Gus wasn't much for sentimental goodbyes. "I best skeedaddle—fixin' to make this long trip o'er yonder. Home is 250 miles as the crow flies, ya know."

"Soooooo looooooong," came the next farewell. Mortimer Moose was also an animal of few words.

After many months, Dolby was still learning new phrases from his exotic friends. Canuck carried a pack on his back and was about to head north when he stopped. "How's she bootin'er, eh?"

"Huh?" Dolby replied.

"'How's she bootin'er'—you know—how's life treatin' ya; how's it going?"

"Oh! Everything's fine. I'm sure going to miss you all though." Dolby felt the waterworks starting.

"Oh, hey, listen would'ya? A nice warm chinook may blow us together someday. In the meantime, I'll be out and aboot remembering my old friend Dolby." Dolby hugged Canuck goodbye.

"Alvita, good Dolby," Saluja, the Sambar buck joined the parade of send-offs.

Zayan was with him and added in a quick cadence, "It was our pleasure to fight alongside the great Half-tail. We are ever in your debt." They bowed, turned, and departed.

The next to say their good-byes were Yukon and Nanuk, the imposing Caribou. Only instead of a farewell greeting, Yukon spoke just one word— "Come." Dolby followed Yukon on the worn trail, with Nanuk bringing up the rear. He figured that this would be his last conversation with Fantasma Bianca. Already emotional, Dolby did not want this to be it—he wanted to continue to be the great Half-tail of the whitetail. He wanted to be able to seek advice from Fantasma anytime he wanted as before. He wanted his treehouse back. He wanted his Mom back. Tears began to flow even before he saw the majestic Albino deer. He wasn't ready for all of this to go away. When Dolby first caught a glimpse of the snowy fur atop the highest rock of the Ring of Nod, he couldn't contain himself. He ran full-speed, and full-wailing, toward the standing doe. Out of habit, the two caribou chased behind him, and six others appeared from the brush in full protection mode. They were prepared to shield Fantasma at all costs. Knowing this, Fantasma gave a wave of her front hoof to call off the pursuit. It didn't occur to Dolby in his sorrow that he was not allowed on the top of the ring—nobody was allowed but Her Wisdom. He climbed up anyway, threw his arms around her legs and continued to sob. Through what Geema called "the schnooks," Dolby, like one of his rapid-fire fireworks, cried out with question after question—so quickly that it wasn't possible to answer.

"What am I going to do without you? Where will you be? Will I ever be needed as a half-tail again? Will I ever see you again? Will I ever see the rest of my friends again? Why does it have to be this way?"

Fantasma was able to calm the boy down by kneeling on her front legs before him. She replied in a soothing tone. "The answer to all your questions . . ."

Dolby quickly regained his composure and interrupted, "Is the Windmaster. I know—sorry."

"Actually, I was going to say, 'you will survive,' 'where I am needed,' 'not sure,' 'maybe,' 'maybe,' and 'not sure!'"

Dolby's head made a double-take. "Wait. What?"

Her laughter at her own joke relaxed Dolby. "Of course, the answer to all of your questions is The Windmaster! You have answered well. The hard part is to trust that the winds that are sent your way come through the wise and good Master of the Winds. Remember, young Half-tail, that even if you are not needed as a half-tail, that doesn't mean that you cease to be one. You have been made and named Half-tail—that will never change. You remain Half-tail always." Dolby sensed that there was nothing more to be said. After one more squeeze, Dolby stepped down the stony steps to the ground where Snowflake awaited. Just as they were about to leave the secluded area, he heard another sound from behind him. "Oh, and Dolby?" It was the sweet voice of Fantasma once more. "Thank your mother for us," and with that, she climbed down and disappeared into the brush. Confused, Dolby turned and ran to ask her what she meant, but it was too late—she was gone. Dolby threw a look of confusion Snowflake's way, who had the same look on her face.

"Maybe she thought you lived with your mom and not Geema?" Snowflake wondered.

"Or maybe she wanted me to thank Mom for moving me to Gomer last year?" speculated Dolby.

"Yeah, that's it. That must be it," the fawn replied. Snowflake knew that Dolby was going to be down after saying goodbye to his friends, so she proceeded with her idea of how to cheer him up. "Dolby?"

"Yeah?"

"Come with me. I've got a surprise for you!"

38

REBUILDING

"'Why did you do all this for me?' Wilbur asked. 'I don't deserve it.
I've never done anything for you.'
'You have been my friend,' replied Charlotte.
'That in itself is a tremendous thing.'"

—*E.B. White in Charlotte's Web (1952)*

Dolby broke the silent walk through the woods. "Snowflake?"
"Yes?"

"I have to admit—I'm kind of hurt. Shadow Muzzle never said good-bye—and I thought we were close. Did you see him leave?"

"I did not, and I haven't seen him in a while," answered the deer.

As the young doe led him through the woods, Dolby was at least grateful that Snowflake wasn't leaving. But he was realistic—he knew that Snowflake would grow up, leave his house, start a family, and grow out of their friendship. "Where are we going?" Dolby asked. He was glad for the diversion. Ever since the operation ended, he craved excitement.

"You'll see!" Snowflake answered in a sing-song voice.

"Come on! Just tell me. Where are we going?" Dolby realized they were nearing the ashes of his beloved treehouse. "Snowflake! Where are we going?" There was no answer. Dolby stopped, turned around, and scanned the forest. The deer was nowhere to be found.

"Aw, come on!" Dolby shouted, "NOT AGAIN! You know I hate when you do this!" He guessed that he was supposed to keep walking along the path, until he knew he was supposed to—when he heard voices and pounding up ahead. Dolby's curiosity got the best of him and he began to jog toward the noises. The path opened up to a small clearing, where some familiar faces and voices were all working hard on different parts of something that took Dolby completely by surprise.

"DOLBY! What are you doing here? You weren't supposed to see this until we were done!" yelled Adele. "But—oh, well—since you're here . . . welcome to your new treehouse!"

Dolby's jaw fell open and it stayed there. Before his eyes was a massive structure tucked away between two giant oak trees—at least three times the size of the first tree blind. Steele was nailing on the last of the roof shingles and yelled from atop a ladder, "We haven't finished staining it—but it's all yours, Dough-boy!"

Jed Calhoun and Clay Brown popped out at the same time to see his reaction. "Come on, old boy! Try 'er out for size!" Adele motioned for him to follow her. She led him up two stories of steps with railings, which was a major upgrade from the old blind's ladder nailed to the tree. The steps emptied onto a wrap-around deck that overlooked 360 degrees of the woods. It was built around two trees that extended up through holes in the deck and formed braces for the walls of the house. Dolby walked around the entire balcony and soaked in the views from each side. On the back side, connected to the deck, was a swinging, suspension bridge. Dolby crossed over to find a circular platform under the cover of another large tree. In the middle of this patio sat an all-weather bean bag chair next to a table made out of a tree stump.

"It's for reading your comic books, I mean for doing homework," laughed Adele. There was even a zip line to the ground to use in order to exit the second deck. He couldn't believe this was his! He was enjoying the balcony so much that he had to be reminded to check out the inside. He cautiously navigated the bridge again, and then entered the house through a full-sized front door, surrounded on both sides by full-sized windows. The men and kids followed him inside.

"500 square feet!" exclaimed a proud Jed. Inside, a gas generator hummed as it powered a variety of electric appliances and "necessities." The most obvious one was a circular fireplace in the middle of the room, which was already bright with fake fire and real heat for the chilly winter day. Dolby tried not to think of the last time he saw flames in a treehouse. A makeshift kitchen was at the back of the open space, complete with a small refrigerator and cabinets fully stocked with expired Frito-Lay products, courtesy of Steele. On the right, along the wall, were a set of bunk beds for slumber parties.

"You did this for me? I can't even believe it. Thank you all so much," choked Dolby.

"We were hoping it might be for us, too!" said Steele with a smirk. "After all, we have been working on it for almost three weeks." His comment made Dolby put two-and-two together.

"That's why you were too busy to hang out with me!"

"We all decided it was the least we could do after all you did to expose the Krantz's and protect the Gomer deer," Adele explained. Dolby exited the treehouse and took one more spin around the overlook.

He stopped, turned his head to the side like Zeke would do, and asked, "Hey! Is that Mr. Canis? What's he working on?" Swampy Canis was a good 500 yards ahead in the middle of a barren cornfield with screwdriver in hand. Adele was only all too happy to show him.

"Come on! You're gonna like this, too!" When they got closer, Swampy was putting the finishing turns on a locking mechanism of a small wooden shed.

"Hey Dolby! She's a real beauty, ain't she?" Dolby didn't know if he was talking about the treehouse or the shed.

"What's this all about?" asked Dolby.

"This? Oh, see for yourself." Swampy stepped away and Dolby pulled open the door of what looked like a small tool shed. Inside were stacked pallets of shrink-wrapped fireworks! Dolby about fell over. There were bottle rockets, firecrackers, Roman Candles, Jumping Jacks, Cherry Bombs, smoke bombs—more fireworks than Dolby had ever seen in one place. He inspected the varieties of fireworks like a kid in a candy store. He fought back tears once again.

"I . . . I . . . don't know what to say."

"Say that you love it!" said Steele.

"Say that you won't tell Officer Robinson or Kowalski!" said Jed with a wink.

"And that you'll only shoot them off out here in the open!" added Adele. They all laughed, having learned the story behind how the first tree fort was destroyed.

"Oh, don't worry—I'm going to take good care of my new place! Thanks again everyone."

The sun was setting on an emotionally exhausting day. The work had wrapped up for the day at the new tree house, which Dolby now affectionately called Hart Castle. He had just recently learned from Geema that the word *hart* that also served as his last name was a synonym for a male deer. Hart and buck and stag were used interchangeably. It was another of the many Windmaster "coincidences" that Dolby marveled at. As he headed home toward the bridge, Snowflake popped out of the brush to join him.

"Hey! How long have you known about the tree fort and why didn't you tell me?" needled Dolby.

"I've known for a while," answered the deer. "We whitetail can be sneaky when we want to be!"

At that second, they were startled by an explosion of branches to their right that caused them to jump back. A massive black figure hurtled its mass in front of them as if being shot out of a cannon hidden in a cluster of pine trees. "DON'T DO THAT!" sighed Dolby. It was Shadow Muzzle. It didn't help that that the woods were now almost pitch black with darkness.

His low, booming voice responded with, "Blacktail sneaky too!" Dolby and Snowflake breathed deeply to recover from their scare. Despite the shock, he was happy to see the buck.

"I thought you had left without saying goodbye."

"Shadow no leave—stay in Gomer. Half-tail will see more of blacktail."

"You're not leaving with the rest? That's awesome! What made you decide to stick around?" Dolby was grateful to hear the good news but felt tired at the same time from the day's roller coaster ride of emotions.

"Shadow Muzzle job—guard Half-tail. That not change. Shadow stay—watch for danger. Shadow like being Half-tail's shadow!" Dolby threw his arms around the massive stag. "Shadow walk you home now—have feeling night not over for Half-tail."

39

VISITORS

"The cunning of the fox is as murderous as the violence of the wolf."

—*THOMAS PAINE*

Shadow said goodnight as Dolby and Snowflake forced open the sliding glass door. Geema greeted them with a, "Well, hello strangers! You've been gone all day—there's pizza and acorns on the oven." The two friends helped themselves, with absolutely no idea that anything had changed. Geema was watching some old-timey movie while cradling something. They were paying attention only to their plates, when Geema got sick of waiting for them to notice. "See who I've got here?" It was typical for Geema to take in a stray cat or nurse an injured rabbit back to health—but this was different. Dolby threw down his plate when he finally realized. "This is Kit—it's Japanese for fox." Geema was cuddling with an orange and white baby fox. Dolby jumped onto the couch and began petting the fox pup. Dolby asked Geema a question with a cutesy, baby voice.

"Awwww! Where did you get him?"

"That's a long story—and unfortunately, I can't exactly tell you quite yet." Geema's answer wasn't very convincing.

"Aw, come on! I can tell you want to tell me!"

"I really can't—I shouldn't."

"You have to! What's the story?"

"Okay." Even Dolby was surprised she gave in so quickly. She wanted to see his reaction as much as he wanted to hear the news. "But, if I tell you, there are some major ground rules."

"Anything—you name it!"

"You have to keep this quiet."

"That's easy. I won't tell a soul."

"No, I said it the wrong way. You actually have to remain quiet."

"I'm confused," replied Dolby, "I have to be quiet? Where? In the house?"

"Yes. I'm about to show you something that will make you happy—but you can't be loud about it."

"Okaaaay."

"So, there's some really good news, but some not-so-good news, too."

"What's the good news?"

"Come with me—I have to show you." Geema set Kit down on the couch, who continued to cuddle against the couch pillow. She led them to the laundry room. She turned and put her finger to her lips—"Sssssshhhhhhhh." She slowly opened the door, revealing a large dog bed with seven baby red foxes curled up around a mother fox. Geema let them see, then quietly closed the door.

"I'm still confused. Where did these foxes come from?" Dolby asked.

"I'm not done with the good news yet. But remember, it is really important that you remain quiet. Do you remember me telling you about my grandfather Clarence Withers?"

"The one who was half-tail fox?"

"That's the one." She walked them over to the guest bedroom. "Well, what I didn't tell you was that he isn't the only one in our family who is a half-tail to the fox species." She opened the bedroom door in the same cautious way and whispered, "Look what the wind blew in!" Inside, asleep on the bed, was Dolby's mother! Dolby was about to yell "Mom!" and rush in, when he heard a loud, alarming moan from the pile of blankets. Geema made the universal sign for "Ssshhh" again as she quietly closed the door.

"Mom's home!" whispered Dolby. "Is she okay?" It finally sank in what his Grandmother was saying. "Wait. My mom is a fox half-tail?"

"That's right, dear. But I really can't say any more than that. I think it'd be better if she was the one to catch you up to speed."

"But is she okay?"

"Well, that's the bad news. She is quite weak and ill."

"Is it . . . is it . . . drugs?" He had heard the rumors.

Geema smiled halfheartedly. "No. It's not drugs. But, I really can't tell you any more right now, child. Let's just be thankful that she is home safe." Dolby noticed that she didn't end her sentence with the usual "safe and sound." The scene in the guest bedroom was sobering enough to halt his curiosity for the moment. Talk about roller coaster rides, Dolby thought. First, he finds out that his mom has returned, and the very next second, he is told she is very ill. He didn't even have time to celebrate. "It's been a long day. Time for you to hit the hay, young man." Dolby hesitated and hung his head in a weak attempt to hide the tears welling up in his eyes. After a few moments of gathering the courage, he pleadingly looked up at his grandma and didn't have to say a word. She understood what he was asking. Geema nodded and against her better judgment said, "go ahead," as the door slowly creaked back open. Dolby couldn't wait that long. He pushed open the door and barged in with tears now streaming down his face.

"MOM! MOM! YOU'RE HOME!" Dolby jumped into bed and the two latched onto one another in a bear hug that was unequal in strength—Dolby's squeeze being far more vigorous—and continued until they both fell asleep. His mom was clearly in pain, and still hadn't said anything. But, she didn't need to. They were home together at last and safe in each other's arms.

Dolby's thoughts about his mom and her illness kept him from sleeping very soundly. He awoke unusually early in the morning and tried to fall back asleep, but soon gave up and left the bedroom. Geema was in the kitchen making a big breakfast. "Is she going to be okay?" he asked. Geema jumped out of her skin at the sound of his voice—she hadn't heard him get up.

"Oh, Dolby—you're gonna give an old lady a heart attack!"

"Is Mom gonna be okay?"

"I think she's going to be alright, but it may take a while. She has been through a lot. Dr. DeWaal thinks it's just exhaustion and the migraines are from dehydration. She's been drinking more water, and took some pain medicine, so maybe we can avoid a hospital stay. He is kind enough to stop by later this morning. It's still really early—why don't you go upstairs and try to catch a few more winks?"

"But I'm not gonna be able to sleep."

"Would it help if I filled in some blanks for you? I'm not sure your Mom would mind—it could be awhile before she can fill you in anyway."

40

SACRIFICE

"Each species, be it a form of bacteria or deer, is knitted together in a network of interdependence, however indirect the links may be."

—*MURRAY BOOKCHIN IN THE ECOLOGY OF FREEDOM (1982)*

Geema and Dolby talked for hours about his Mom and what she had been through, leaving Dolby feeling amazed and loved and ashamed all at the same time. His Mom did recover later that March, but only after a lot of rest and a lot of Geema's home cooking. She just needed a stress-free existence, and to know that her son was safe and well. I know this, because I am Dolby's Mom. My name is Karen Withers-Hart.

You may wonder what Mom—I mean, Geema—told Dolby that morning. Well, here are some highlights. After the tree hit the house that night and we were forced to move to Gomer, it was a very difficult time. My husband had left, I had lost my job, and my health was a question mark. All I had left was Dolby and Mother. But, as it turned out, I was in a place in life that gave me the freedom to leave and do what I had to do. A coincidence, you ask? I think not. I couldn't tell Dolby because he wouldn't have understood. I grew up watching my Great-Grandpa Clarence raise, play with, and talk to foxes. Somewhere along the line, I began to understand their conversations. I listened in on their discussions. By the time I was in high school, I was just like my Great-Grandpa—a full blown half-tail to the fox race. I kept this from Dolby all these years because it has been obvious since he was small that he was a friend of the deer. I knew from my family that it was important for nature to run its course on these things and for him to learn it in his own time. It was only after moving to Gomer that the chatter began. Because fox and coyote are related species, the fox in this area began to hear and share the rumors and news about the threat to the whitetail from coyote. Knowing that Dolby, as the only half-tail to the deer, was about to be in the middle of something very dangerous and even life-threatening, I made the difficult decision to leave Dolby behind with his Geema. Why did I leave? What was I doing the whole time? All good questions. I became singularly obsessed with my son's safety. Of course, now that I know he was protected, I regret none of it. It was like something took over. I slept very little and didn't take care of myself—all for the sake of my son. In fact, I lost over twenty-five pounds in the last six months. I departed with my fox friends in order to recruit the best fighting stags to Gomer and to Dolby's side that the deer species had to offer. Some of them, of course, didn't need my persuasion. As they say, the Windmaster was already guiding them here. I guess you can say that I simply used all of my resources to bring more help in order to increase my son's odds. I traveled to California, Oregon, Washington, Canada—you name it—anywhere that I could to find help. You may wonder how this was possible, given that I can only speak fox. One thing you have to understand is that even though animals can't directly communicate verbally with one another, they do have the unique ability to communicate non-verbally—and somehow my message for help didn't get lost in translation. So, nothing that I said to Dolby on the night that I left was a lie. I did have to leave because of my love for him. I could not help him here. I could only help him elsewhere. I did leave for him. As for seeing him again? I encountered some dangerous situations—I really wasn't sure if I'd be back. The only thing I was sure of was that I had to do everything in my power to protect him back home in Gomer, even if it killed me. And, honestly, it almost did.

One last story from school on the Monday after I returned home. Things were back to normal, with Dolby back to being a nobody. Kids throughout the day called him Dough-boy as usual—the nickname had unfortunately stuck. Even Steele continued to use that slur when talking to him. Only

Steele took Dolby aside later and told him that it may sound like he's calling him Dough-boy, but he really was not anymore. Dolby knew what he heard and was confused. Steele proceeded to tell him that he was no longer calling him Dough-boy, but another nickname that sounded like it. "Every time you hear me say your name," he told him, "I don't want you to think I'm calling you the same old thing. From now on, you may hear 'Dough-boy' but what I'm really saying is 'Doe-boy'—D-O-E boy, like the female deer. It is my way, instead of insulting you, to show you respect. I would suggest that whenever you also hear the insult from others, you think only of my nickname—because it is the truth about who you really are, whether anybody else knows it or not. You know it, and the Windmaster knows it—what other opinion matters?"

I don't tell you all of this so that you will think highly of me or my son. Dolby's willingness to sacrifice out of love for his friends, and my willingness to sacrifice out of love for my son, is not all that extraordinary. Regular people everywhere live their lives sacrificing for the ones they love. Soldiers in the military have been doing it forever. You might do the same if you are ever placed in the position we were. I think it's because we are all made in God's image—each as unique as snowflakes—that we have the capacity to love like He does. Because after all, His Son was the first half-tail—if I can say it like that. Only that in His case, He was fully God and fully man all at the same time. Think about it—Jesus left heaven to become man to speak to men and women on behalf of God. He was the mediator who actually did go to his death to save the ones He loved. He then rose again from the dead, conquering death to prove He was God. A wise man once said that there is no greater love than when one sacrifices his own life for his friends. That's what Jesus did! In light of all of that, each of us has a decision to make. Are we going to trust ourselves and our own abilities to know the Windmaster and earn eternal life? You see how well that worked for Dolby at first. Or, are we going to trust that Jesus made both a way to God and salvation possible through his death on the cross in our place? Either Jesus pays for our sins, or we will pay for our sins one day. I'm not sure if Dolby is quite there yet, although he is putting much more faith in the Windmaster than ever before.

I also don't know what is in store for us as a family, or even for Dolby as a half-tail. I don't speak Windmaster after all—only fox. He alone knows. But, we will continue as half-tails following the original Half-tail.

"For there is one God, and there is one mediator between God and men,

the man Christ Jesus, who gave himself as a ransom for all."

—1 TIMOTHY 2:5–6

www.ingramcontent.com/pod-product-compliance
Lightning Source LLC
Chambersburg PA
CBHW051527050726
47503CB00014B/2051